I was trapped in my offi[illegible] the review copy of “Pop a Yellow Smoke” that Chuck Truitt sent me. It was a great read. As I read each account, memories returned and you realize at my advanced age this period was a very defining point in my life.

Chuck’s account of his experience made it real. Too often we read books which frankly try to “tell a story,” not talk about “true life experience.” Chuck tells it the way it was. Often dull and boring, but always dangerous—this was Vietnam as we knew it.

I was captured by his hunt for rats so maybe a trip to the “Orkin Man” is in order, or a call to the Patent Office.

Chuck continues to tell our story, and continues to serve our fellow man. He truly rates being called “Forever a Marine—Forever One of the Finest!”

As always, I’m Semper Fi

James E Livingston
Major General, U.S.M.C. (Ret)
MOH (Medal of Honor recipient)

“Right on Target.” A book which artfully mixes the devastating reality of the Vietnam war with hard-hitting humor that will be well received by all, especially the combat veteran. Chuck Truitt’s personal firsthand experiences of the war and its tragedies is balanced well with those images all veterans seek—distant memories of comrades-in-arms and good times, long misplaced but not forgotten. A truly inspiring book for the Christian and non-Christian alike.

As a retired Marine officer, combat veteran (Beirut 1983) and a member of Pastor Truitt’s missionary church on Okinawa from 1993-96, I can personally attest to his steadfast dedication to the Marine Corps, all veterans and, more importantly, his unwavering commitment to our Lord and Saviour, Jesus Christ.

Respectfully submitted,

Kenneth W. Keverline
LtCol USMC, Retired

These veterans have already read the book:

"...I have said all along Chuck Truitt has a natural talent for penmanship and his stories have been detailed and interesting. His book will be an inspiration for all of us who have since shared forgotten memories and exploits. The past year's discussions and reunions with those who served in the 1st Radio Battalion have proven to be a stimulating catharsis for long-ago experiences we all share today, but lived with privately over the past 35 years."

Rob Charnell, Sgt., USMC, RVN 69–70

"I found that the mention of certain words, locations and phrases brought back long-repressed memories stored in the back of my brain, which brought many hours of joyful reminiscing. For me, the readings were therapeutic."

Carl Daigle, Sgt., USMC, RVN 69–70

"More memoir than war story, Chuck Truitt's well-written reminiscences of his experiences in Vietnam relate the humor, the fear and the sadness that all Vietnam vets will remember. Reading this took me back to a time and place I'll always remember, and recalls names and faces I'll never forget."

Jim Barton, SSgt., USMC, RVN 66–67

"I like to think that I gave Chuck a lot of encouragement while he was writing this book. Very few books are written about the type of work we did in the Radio Battalions, and probably none written about the 1st Radio Battalion in Vietnam. Most of what we accomplished was done with the proverbial 'shoestring' and a group of the most dedicated Marines that could ever be assembled during the Vietnam war. Chuck's story is really the story of all the Marines that served in the 1st Radio Battalion, and I had the privilege of serving with many of them during the year I was there. Thanks, Chuck, for writing our story."

George Carnako, Capt., USMC, Retired, RVN 69–70

"After being 'back in the world' for nearly 33 years, your stories were an enjoyable trip down memory lane for me. You rekindled long-dormant memories of an experience that I once shared briefly but intensely with a crazy yet motivated and dedicated band of Marine 'spooks.' I especially enjoyed your stories of our friend, Greek. Thanks for remembering him."

Tim Lundberg, Sgt., USMC, RVN 69–71

"These are the kinds of stories I like to read when I think of Vietnam. They are about the closer-than-family friendships that were developed in a very short time, and they recall the 'adventures' we all want to share rather than the 'events' we'd just as soon forget. The acronyms and equipment nomenclature Chuck uses will bring a story to each of our minds that we thought we had forgotten. I completely enjoyed the description of the day-to-day fight against the boredom and the elements every Marine faced during his tour. In the end Chuck has discovered and described a time when each of us stepped away from innocence and into accountability, and he was able to do it with a twinkle in his eye that all of us 'vets' cherish and try to keep kindled."

Will Easley, SSgt., USMC, RVN 69–71

"Chuck Truitt has never outgrown being a young Marine at heart. It makes both his ministry and his writing alive. It is very important for men and women who have served together in a combat zone to read and reminisce periodically about those experiences. It is good for the heart and, along with time it helps heal hurts, wounds and longings that those who have not fought for freedom will ever really understand. Chuck also offers some good advice from God's Word on several important issues. God's Word can heal the sinsick soul of any soldier, sailor, airman or Marine [veteran, civilian, etc.] who simply comes to the Lord by faith. It is my prayer that God will use this book to encourage, inform and witness for the Captain of our salvation."

Kimble D. Stohry, Colonel, USAF, Retired -A/OA-10 Pilot

FROM A COMBAT
VETERAN MARINE
VIETNAM, 1969-1970

POP A YELLOW SMOKE

AND OTHER MEMORIES!

W. Charles Truitt

ACW Press
Ozark, AL 36360

Scripture quotations are taken from the King James Version of the Bible.

Pop a Yellow Smoke

Cover Design by Alpha Advertising
Interior Design by Pine Hill Graphics

Packaged by ACW Press
1200 HWY 231 South #273
Ozark, AL 36360
www.acwpress.com
The views expressed or implied in this work do not necessarily reflect those of ACW Press. Ultimate design, content, and editorial accuracy of this work is the responsibility of the author(s).

Library of Congress Cataloging-in-Publication Data
(Provided by Cassidy Cataloguing Services, Inc.)

Truitt, W. Charles (Wesley Charles), 1949-

Pop a yellow smoke and other memories : from a combat veteran Marine--Vietnam, 1969-1970 / W. Charles Truitt. -- 1st ed. -- Ozark, AL : ACW Press, 2005.

p. ; cm.
ISBN: 1-932124-52-7

1. Vietnamese Conflict, 1961-1975--Personal narratives.
2. Vietnamese Conflict, 1961-1975--Military intelligence.
3. Vietnamese Conflict, 1961-1975--Veterans--Biography. I. Title.

DS559.5 .T78 2005
959.704/3/092--dc22 0504

Printed in the United States of America.

In dedication to, and with thanks:

This book is in dedication to, and with thanks to, all the men of the 1st Radio Battalion who served our great country fighting the spread of communism in the Republic of South Vietnam.

By changing the names around, these could be nearly the same stories for many of the other Marines of the battalion.

Thank you Rick, George, Joe, Pineapple, Carl, Will, Bob and the other battalion veterans who encouraged me to put these stories into a book. Our children can now know what we did, and won't have to think of us as war criminals, baby killers and the many other false images we have been portrayed as being. You and I know that we served honorably, and with honorable intent. We did our jobs, and did them in an exemplary manner. Some of our friends died doing the same thing. Now our children can have confidence in us.

Though most of these pictures are my own, I certainly want to give my sincere thanks to those Marines who have allowed me to use theirs, as well as the very few pictures that were acquired from other sources.

What Did You Do in the War, Grandpa

This book, these stories have been written to answer questions for my children and grandchildren. They are written as honest and straightforward as I can remember everything from my tour with 1st Radio Battalion in 1969–1970. These stories have been cleaned up and sanitized, for the readers and have not included all the gory, gross stuff. The point of view is from 1st Radio Battalion's Signals Intelligence/Communications Security mission. We were Marines, but we worked a little different from the bulk of most military units in Vietnam. That doesn't mean anything other than that my stories bring another aspect of America's involvement in Vietnam.

For 14 years I served the Marines on active duty, the last three as a gunnery sergeant, at which time I left the Corps to attend Tennessee Temple University in Chattanooga, Tennessee, in preparation for full- time Christian work. For over 17 years now I have lived and worked on Okinawa as a missionary/pastor of a Baptist church, mainly to the American military. Actually, I am still a Marine at heart, just with a different Commanding Officer.

"A good man leaveth an inheritance
to his children's children...."
Proverbs 13:22

In remembrance of those 1st Radio Battalion Marines who unabashedly, and with no qualms or misgivings, honorably served their country to fight communism in the Republic of Vietnam.

Know this guys, we drained the communist resolve, and from the time of the Vietnam conflict forward, communism began a worldwide regression; less than 20 years later, even the giant Soviet Union collapsed.

JAMES WESTLEY AYERS was born on October 31, 1934, and joined the Armed Forces while in Moncks Corner, South Carolina. He served as a 2502 in the Marine Corps. In ten years of service, he attained the rank of CAPT/O3. On May 26, 1967, at the age of 32, Jim perished in the service of our country in South Vietnam, Quang Tin. He is honored on the Vietnam Veterans Memorial on Panel 20E, Row 110.

STEPHEN LEE TRAUGHBER was born on April 17, 1946, and joined the Armed Forces while in New Albany, Indiana. He served as a 2575 in the Marine Corps. In two years of service, he attained the rank of CPL/E4. On September 10, 1967, at the age of 21, Steve perished in the service of our country in South Vietnam, Quang Tri. He is honored on the Vietnam Veterans Memorial on Panel 26E, Row 52.

LARRY ALLAN JONES was born on July 28, 1948, and joined the Armed Forces while in Thousand Oaks, California. He served as a 2571 in the Marine Corps. In one year of service, he attained the rank of LCPL/E3. On April 24, 1968, at the age of 19, Larry perished in the service of our country in South Vietnam, Quang Tri. He is honored on the Vietnam Veterans Memorial on Panel 51E, Row 47.

WALTER JAMES DANCER was born on July 17, 1945 and joined the Armed Forces while in FORT LAUDERDALE, FL. He served as a 3300 in the Marine Corps. In 4 years of service, he attained the rank of CPL/E4. On May 3, 1968, at the age of 22, Walter perished in the service of our country in South Vietnam, Quang Nam. You can find Walter honored on the Vietnam Veterans Memorial on Panel 54E, Row 24.

WILLIAM IVAN INMAN was born on January 22, 1944, and joined the Armed Forces while in Chardon, Ohio. He served as a 3531 in the Marine Corps. In four years of service, he attained the rank of CPL/E4. On May 3, 1968, at the age of 24, Bill perished in the service of our country in South Vietnam, Quang Nam. He is honored on the Vietnam Veterans Memorial on Panel 54E, Row 25.

PAUL JAY KINGERY was born on April 24, 1946, and joined the Armed Forces while in Chardon, Ohio. He served as a 2571 in the Marine Corps. In four years of service, he attained the rank of SGT/E5. On May 13, 1968, at the age of 22, Paul perished in the service of our country in South Vietnam, Quang Nam. He is honored on the Vietnam Veterans Memorial on Panel 59E, Row 25.

EDWARD REYNOLD STORM was born on January 8, 1930, and joined the Armed Forces while in Portland, Oregon. He served as a 2578 in the Marine Corps. In 20 years of service, he attained the rank of MGYS/E9. On December 28, 1969, at the age of 39, Ed perished in the service of our country in South Vietnam, Quang Nam. He is honored on the Vietnam Veterans Memorial on Panel 15W, Row 105.

LARRY WADE DUKE was born on January 31, 1948, and joined the Armed Forces while in Summerville, Georgia. He served as a 2571 in the Marine Corps. In three years of service, he attained the rank of SGT/E5. On March 10, 1970, at the age of 22, Larry perished in the service of our country in South Vietnam, Quang Nam. He is honored on the Vietnam Veterans Memorial on Panel 13W, Row 103.

ROBERT HRISOULIS, "Greek," was born on November 27, 1950, and joined the Armed Forces while in Detroit, Michigan. He served as a 2571 in the Marine Corps. In two years of service, he attained the rank of SGT/E5. On January 21, 1971, at the age of 20, Greek perished in the service of our country in South Vietnam, Quang Nam. He is honored on the Vietnam Veterans Memorial on Panel 5W, Row 58.

Contents

And so, I give you
my children and grandchildren,

A History Lesson

Starting With The Cold War

When our great nation declared itself independent, it was the only democracy anywhere in the world. Shortly thereafter, the British Parliament finally won control of the monarchy, which made Great Britain a closely following second democracy. Now, a little over 200 years later—a scant fraction in the history of the world—democracy of some type is the eminent form of government in most nations around the entire globe. After WW II the violent global expansion of communism was a very real threat to democracy everywhere. Truman's 1947 speech concerned the establishment of the Truman Doctrine of containing communist expansion. America had to stop it, no one else would, or could. Communist North Vietnam was determined to conquer noncommunist South Vietnam. President Kennedy spoke precisely of that in his letter ("our primary purpose is to help your people maintain their independence") to President Diem of South Vietnam in 1961.

North Vietnam lost nearly two million of its brightest and most capable young men in the effort to forcefully overthrow South Vietnam. America had effectively checked that advance and drained the communist nations supplying and financing that effort at the cost of some 58,000 of her finest young men. After the U.S. was gone with victory in 1973, and a viable noncommunist government firmly in power, the Communist North resumed their efforts in the south in 1975. Then, after finally achieving their goal of forceful domination, they murdered tens of thousands of people who had opposed them, and incarcerated hundreds of thousands in re-education camps.

So, Why Did America Become Entangled in the Vietnamese Web?

At the end of WW II, the expansion of communism was swift, meteoric in fact. America's leadership was appallingly conscious of the communist expansion, and America was the only democracy with the combination of ability and backbone to act in opposition to it. You have to remember that most democracies were themselves fighting to survive after the devastation of WW II.

I came across a great apologetic by Chuck Gutzman, who can be read on the internet. I like how he puts it here in this particular section:

> *Get a map of the world as it was at the outbreak of WWII and consider this – (In fact, to really get the point color the communist powers and their conquests red). At the outbreak of the Second World War in 1939 there was only one Communist State, the Soviet Union. At the end of WWII Europe was prostrate, with most of her industrial capacity shattered and literally millions unsure as to how they were going to cope with whatever came next. By the end of 1945 Latvia, Lithuania, Estonia, Poland, Romania, Bulgaria, and Hungary had all been absorbed by the red army. Germany and Korea had been divided in two, and East Prussia disappeared from the maps of the world forever. Finland was forced into tenuous neutrality though, because of her proximity, she tended to support Russian causes when asked to. The British, Dutch, and French overseas empires were disintegrating, with the Dutch being the first to go.*

> *In Indochina Ho Chi Minh, who had been one of the founders of the French Communist Party, and was the founder of the Indochinese Communist Party, was engaged with the French. The Red Chinese were slugging it out with the Kuomintang in China, the Hukbalapaps were becoming active in the Philippines, and Yugoslavia, a loose amalgam of the former countries of Bosnia, Herzegovina, Slovenia, Montenegro, Macedonia, Croatia, and Serbia was in the throes of determining how they would organize as a communist state.*

In my own way, I want to put down a synopsis here of some of the things that caused us to go to Vietnam. Between 1945 and 1949 the communists continued to expand, practically in an unchecked manner. Southeast Asia was a clear objective of the communists. During that time (1947) the Marshall Plan was enacted to help devastated countries. After Roosevelt's death on 12 April 1945, President Truman was acutely aware of the "Red" scourge that was acting as a juggernaut and swallowing countries by design. He introduced his Truman Doctrine in 1947 to counter the communist expansion.

Let's back up just a tad. During the war, in order to motivate the American population to provide War Materiel, the USSR—and on its coattails, communism—was made to look like a special place and ally in the fight against fascism. Much of the American movie industry, and many universities, went along, and swallowed that line of thinking; communism, to them, looked especially tempting. And, it can look tempting on paper, but when put to the test, we know communism falls radically short. For instance, the Ukraine was once known as "the breadbasket" of Europe. But, under the communist leadership, the area was known for starvation. Furthermore, the communist's methods counted humanity, by the millions, as but fodder. I saw one poll that had 54 percent of Americans trusting the Russians in September of 1945. By February 1946 a realization of just who they were had dropped the American trust to 35 percent. But many in the movie industry and the colleges still saw communism on paper. Its reality never made a dent on them. To a large extent, the professors' doctrine, spilled over into the college students—in addition to the "rebellious times"—resulted in numerous campus unrest and demonstrations. As far as the movie industry goes, have you ever heard of a pro-Vietnam-war film? Although I have seen movies of how unjustly mistreated the industry portrayed itself as being, figure the odds on them showing the truth. Remember, Hanoi Jane was an actress! Granted she was not indicative of them all, to which I say Amen! One can still see in some of them their bent in that direction though. Some of those folks would have been the Tories, and redcoat sympathizers during the War of Independence! General George Patton was right about the Russians and communism much earlier, but he was portrayed as an idiot and wasn't listened to in time.

Looking back into the Far Eastern world situation, Ho Chi Minh and General Vo Nguyen Giap, Ho and Vo, were trained by our OSS, the predecessor to the CIA, to fight the Japanese in WW II. Did you know that Ho was reportedly a fan of Thomas Jefferson and quoted him? It may be that Ho and Vo were just basically Vietnamese Nationalists in the 1920's with the desire of uniting all of Vietnam, and getting them out from under the heavy thumb of the French. Seeking ways to do that, they became enamored with the communist scheme. After WW II was over, Ho petitioned Washington to convince the French to stay out of Vietnam and not try to take over their former colony again. That is certainly understandable since the French had tried to eliminate all nationalism in Vietnam back in the 1920s, (in order to keep it a subservient colony) and in 1930 especially when they imprisoned or murdered hundreds of Vietnamese at the Yen Bay mutiny. But—and this is a big but—after WW II,

Ho and Vo evoked the communist methodology to unite their homeland, even though not all of Vietnam wanted to become communist.

THE COMMUNIST JUGGERNAUT WAS ROLLING

In mainland China, Chang Kai Shek fled to Taiwan from the communist takeover in China in 1949, and of course we know from bloody history that North Korea invaded South Korea in 1950. Southeast Asia continued to be captivated with communists. Even one of the provinces of India embraced communism (one source reported to me there were as many as two to four provinces). The French were "Waterloo'd" by the communist forces at Dien Bien Phu in 1954, which we know was in Vietnam. And in 1959, across in the western hemisphere, Cuba's Castro was beating on America's door.

So, where was every other democracy? They were all preoccupied, and/or self-absorbed with the great war weariness of two back-to-back world wars. That weariness continued up into the 1960s.

So, who would stop the communists ubiquitous advance? Would the British do it? No, they were wearily trying to muddle through the chaotic messes of the once great British Empire. Would the French do it? Isn't that a funny thought; remember the weariness of Waterloo, errr Dien Bien Phu! To put it succinctly, the only democratic nation with the guts, the guns, the moxie and the ability to stop the communists was the same nation that had the guts to break away and form the first democracy nearly 200 years earlier.

It was America to the rescue!

GLOSSARY

1st RadBn, the 1st Radio Battalion, 1st Rad Bn or 1st Rag Bag. Its job was the intercept of radio and electronic communications for the purpose of gaining and exploiting intelligence on the enemy (SigInt, EW-ECM). Another aspect was using our abilities to keep the enemy from exploiting our own signals (ComSec & ECCM).

407th RRD, is a U.S. Army Radio Research Detachment (an Army SigInt unit that was part of the ASA).

6-by, is a two-and-one-half-ton military vehicle; also called a multi-fueller and a deuce and a half.

A4, was another name for Con Thien, the base closest to the DMZ.

Arc Light, was a B-52 strike, usually involving three aircraft which were very rarely ever seen as they were high above the clouds. I was always impressed. Once we were warned in advance of an arc light just 1000-1500 meters away on Mutter's Ridge; the ground shook and twigs and dirt fell on us.

Artillery Round, is an artillery projectile of which there are many types. For instance a 105mm round before it's fired pertains to the whole assemblage of the projectile, powder charge and the case. After firing, it refers to the projectile only. The projectile that goes to the target has a fuse on the tip. The types of projectiles are high explosive, white phosphorus (willie peter), anti-personnel flechettes, illumination flares (lume), smoke (chemical) and "butterfly" bomblets. Some other time we'll talk about fuses!

ASA, is the Army Security Agency—a much larger SIGINT/EW unit than any of the Marine Corps units—that contributed to the Army's operations throughout South Vietnam. (Just between you and me, I think those doggies were a less capable and effective unit that tried to do what the Marine's 1st Rad Bn did, but don't tell 'em I said that!) Actually, they were pretty good. Oh, Okay (choke) they were real good. There! I said it!

Barky, was the call sign for USAF Forward Air Control-Airborne in the Northern "I" Corps area after the 3rd Marine Division left Vietnam.

BAS, is a battalion aid station.

Basketball, was the call-sign for a cargo aircraft, such as a C-130 that would orbit overhead and drop large drum-sized flares to provide light. They were called "basketball ships" of which, I believe, an earlier version was called "puff," although that one was a C-47. They could sure linger on station for a long time, and provide continual illumination.

BBs, is a term for supplies—bullets, bandages and beans—or the common term for any and all supplies, inclusive.

Beehive Round, is a round for the M-79 that is like a large shotgun shell. There was a plastic sabot encasing twenty 00-buck lead pellets which were used for patrolling and close work in the heavy foliage that might cause an HE round to detonate too close. They kicked like a mule when fired. For a 105mm howitzer, the beehive was the flechette round.

Blooper, is the Marine slang name for an M-79 gun.

C-2, was a fire support base (big guns too, 8-inch howitzers) on the western side of Leatherneck Square.

CAR, is a combat action ribbon which is kind of a status ribbon for Marines. One can only receive a CAR for receiving and returning enemy fire. That effectively eliminates many folks who may receive fire, such as rocket or artillery, from many miles away. With a rifle or pistol, it's hard to effectively shoot back at an enemy that is dropping large caliber weapons on you from miles away. A CAR generally means the combat action occurred at close quarters. Many Marines who were fired upon, and even wounded, never really qualified for a CAR. Furthermore, the CAR is generally reserved for Marines engaged in ground combat. For example, Marine aviators would qualify for the "air medal" versus the CAR.

Clacker, is a small green hand-squeeze detonator for blowing up things with blasting caps, such as claymore mines.

Claymore Mine, is an anti-personnel mine first developed at the end of the Korean War. Originally devised by the Germans in WW II as an anti-tank mine, it was refined by the Americans, and ended up having 700 steel ball bearings in the business side, rather than the solid steel plate that the Germans used. C4 is the explosive.

ComSec, is communications security, primarily monitoring our own communications and devising plans to eliminate exploitation by the enemy.

Con Thien, is the Vietnamese name for A4, which is the base closest to the DMZ.

Concertina, is coiled barbed wire that has sharp little blades with points, rather than the wire barbs that are normally associated with regular barbed wire. The coils are strung with two at the bottom and one on top, or sometimes with three on the bottom, then two; usually then the top coil is left off. Even Paul Bunyan couldn't vault that one.

Corps Area, was the term for an area of operations. Vietnam was divided into four areas militarily, actually five if you include the special zone around the greater Saigon area. Few Marines have ever been to Saigon, except the embassy staff, and HQ types.

CP, stands for command post

C-Rations, were combat rations or meals, also referred to as C's or C-rats.

CS, is a type of tear gas used by the military. It is very strong and potent and causes one's sinuses to erupt. Another variant is CN gas.

CW, stands for continuous wave, which just means morse code.

Dancer, was a code name for the Vietnamese linguists that worked with 1st Rad Bn's Signals Intelligence effort. We became quite attached to them, and they were a real benefit to the mission. I suppose that the communist government executed all or most of those men after the takeover.

Deuce and a half, is a two-and-one-half-ton military vehicle which was also called a multi-fueller and a 6-by.

Deuce Gear, is short for 782 gear, or a Marine's combat gear.

DMZ, the Demilitarized Zone, an area between North Vietnam and South Vietnam. In the middle of it ran the Song Ben Hai river.

Doggie, is a soldier of the U.S. Army, first referred to as such by the American press during WW I. I had a soldier ask me one time, "How come whenever the Marines go by, they bark at me?"

Down South, was a term for Vietnam. Such as, "I absolutely loved my tour in paradise, down south."

FAC, is by Marine definition an aviator assigned to a ground combat arms unit, responsible for the accurate control of friendly air support for the ground unit in which he is assigned. FAC-A is a forward air controller-airborne which is usually a slow and low flying aircraft, OV-1 and OV-10 aircraft especially, to control artillery and aircraft ordinance as it is used against a ground target.

Flechette are small nails with fins that are packed by the thousands into ammunition and fired when the enemy is within very close range. The 105mm flechette rounds fired @6000 darts. The pattern was 300 meters deep, @90 meters wide and in a cone shape. The word "*flechette*" is French, and is literally translated "little arrow."

Field Strip, is to take something apart, not necessarily completely, but basically. For instance, when field stripping a rifle, one would leave the firing mechanism assembly or the bolt parts intact. But, one would "field strip" a cigarette butt so that the tobacco was dissipated and the paper rolled up in a tiny ball, then flicked to the wind. Any filters would be pulled apart into little pieces so that nothing was left.

Free Fire Zone, was any area not under control of the good guys or that did not contain friendlies. Anything that moved in an FFZ was liable to be shot if detected. Permission to shoot didn't have to be obtained first. "Injun Country" was another term that roughly equated to an FFZ.

FSB, is the initials for fire support base, a temporary base set up to provide artillery support and to rain down artillery rounds on confirmed or suspected enemy locations. They were usually armed with 4 or 6 howitzers of 105mm, as those guns and their ammunition could be transported by helicopter.

Grunt, is an infantry type Marine, also called a ground pounder and a lot of other names.

Gunnery Sergeant, is probably the paradigm rank of a Marine sergeant. A "gunny" knows just about everything there is to know about his job. After being a gunny, everything else is just icing on the cake. By the way, a grouping of gunnies is called a gaggle. "What the gunny says" is the gospel. That doesn't necessarily hold true for the other services' E7 people, however. In fact, when you have a grouping of E7s from another service, it's probably just a cluster or flock.

HE, is short for high explosive

Helicopter, is not necessarily the same in each service. For the Marines the primary "bird" was a Huey—UH1-E, and the army had a slightly different version of UH1 that they called a slick. The Marines/Navy use the CH-46 Sea Knight, two-bladed chopper, which will fit on the elevators of a ship. The army's two-bladed cargo chopper is a CH-47 chinook (also called a "hook"), which is bigger and stronger, but they don't fit on a ship. For the really heavy lifts, the Marines/Navy have the CH-53 Sea Stallion, and it's a real horse.

H&I, harassment and interdiction was a type of fire (ordinance on target) shot out into a free fire zone, for the purpose of harassing and interdicting enemy activity. Around the perimeter of FSB Fuller, it was a free fire zone at night; we used M-79s for H&I fires.

HFDF, is high frequency direction finding, also just DF, or sometimes called RDF for radio direction finding. The Army also used ARDF, or Airborne Radio Direction Finding which required much more resources, and of course one of their ARDF planes had to be in the vicinity when an enemy radio was transmitting.

Hootch, is a hard backed and sided shelter with an assortment of uses, such as medical facilities, headquarters, dining and clubs, but most important they were fine for quarters. Their size was about 20 feet by 40 or 50 feet and they were often divided into cubicles. They were more stable than tents, and had corrugated tin roofs. Some folks spell the word "hooch," but I personally thought that spelling referred to a slang word for narcotics.

Jane Fonda, is the object of scorn and contempt throughout the Marine Corps, and I'm sure all branches of the U.S. military, AKA Hanoi Jane by every Vietnam veteran. For many years there were decals of Jane Fonda in the urinals of the "O" club at Camp Schwab and the "Eagles Nest" at Courtney, Okinawa. I used to love to "pay my respects" in the head whenever I had a chance to go there.

I Corps, is the northernmost of the four corps areas. The northern border was along the DMZ, the western border was Laos, the eastern border was the South China Sea. Relatively few Marines were ever south of the I Corps area.

KIA, killed in action

KCS, Kit Carson scouts, were former (North Vietnamese Army (NVA) soldiers that were now working for South Vietnam (SVN) and America.

Leatherneck Square, was a part of the Marines tactical area of operational responsibility (TAOR) just below the DMZ. On the north was Con Tien (A4), on the east was Gio Lin, on the south was Dong Ha and Hwy 9, on the west was Cam Lo and Charlie 2. FSB Fuller overlooked Leatherneck Square from the west.

LP, is a listening post, which is a small team of men who go to a different position each night around the perimeter of a camp. Their job is to listen and give the first alarm of impending trouble.

LRPs, long range patrol rations were different than C-rations. With 16 in a carton, and two each of the eight different meals, they were designed to sustain combat troops during the initial assault. They were also for special operations, as well as long-range reconnaissance missions.

LRPs are light at just one pound each, but they require water because they are dehydrated. I really liked them for a change, though we couldn't get them very often.

LZ, is a landing zone, usually for just helicopters.

M-79, is a gun that breaks in the middle and is used to shoot 40mm HE grenades, Beehive/00 Buck, gas, flares and other pyrotechnics; called "thump guns" by the army and "bloopers" by Marines.

Mad Minute, was a defensive tactic when everyone on the perimeter shoots a maximum rate of fire into their own particular defensive zones for a short amount of time. The time is usually determined by a set signal, such as the length of time a pop-up flare burns @45 seconds.

Maddox and Turner Joy, two American Navy destroyers that were attacked by North Vietnam on the high seas of the Tonkin Gulf. Though some question the validity of the event, it did succeed in causing America to have a greater role in the fight against communism.

Marines, for the sake of not using up many, many pages here, let me just say one thing: General John A. Lejeune back in the 1920s or so put out a directive that is still in force, that the word "Marine" will always be capitalized. I once pointed that out to a Navy captain, O-6, but he still scoffingly refused to capitalize Marines in anything he wrote. The Marine general, whom he worked for, eventually canned the guy. I suspect it was for his bull-headed belligerence; after all, isn't bull-headed belligerence the domain of the Marines?

Montagnards, (French for mountain people; see Yards)

MOS, military occupational specialty is a number which designates the specific job for which a person is trained. For instance the 2500 block is communications, the 0800 block is artillery and the 0300 block is infantry. Specifically, a 2531 is a field radio operator, an 0811 is a basic artilleryman and an 0311 is a rifleman. Personally, I held several MOSs, some of which were 2571—special morse code radio operator, 2579—radio direction finder operator and 2574—special radio linguist (French).

Multi-fueller, is a two-and-one-half-ton military vehicle, also called a deuce and a half and a 6-by.

Mutter's Ridge, was an extensive ridge line between Dong Ha mountain and the DMZ. It was the site of many battles over several years. A lot of good men lost their lives there. According to the 1966 volume of the *Marine Corps History of the Vietnam War*, page 195, the ridge was originally named "Mutter Ridge" because "Mutter" was the radio call sign of 3/4 Marines. 3/4 was in heavy combat on the ridge in late September and early October of 1966, as well as the other 4th Marines battalions several times later.

NUG, a new guy, also called by other less complimentary names. Quite often nugs and rear echelon types were indistinguishable in actions and appearance.

NVA, North Vietnamese Army—those were the bad guys!

OIC, officer in charge

OP, outpost

PC, is a term that refers most commonly to platoon commander, as in a PC tent, although a PC vehicle refers to a personnel carrier, a 3/4 ton truck.

Pig, a term for our PRD-1 Radio Direction Finders.

Pig Pen, is where we set up the PRD-1 for operation. Some were in a tent, others were in small, sandbag-enclosed parapets. There was an open area on top so that the directional antenna could rotate and receive unobstructed or undeviated radio waves.

Pop-up, is a small pyrotechnic signal device, usually for flares, and star clusters of different colors.

PRD-1, see Pig.

PSP, is a term for pierced steel planking or runway matting that comes in 16" x 10' sections and each can be attached to the next. It was used to construct a lot of things in addition to runways. I believe it was also called Marston Mat.

Rag Bag, is fond and treasured slang for 1st Rad Bn.

Razorback Ridge, is a torturous, ragged, rocky, convoluted ridge-line that ran in a north-south direction. It was just northwest of the rockpile and west of Dong Ha Mountain.

RDF, radio direction finding

Retreet, is something I'm not sure about, nor am I sure of the correct spelling of this word. It's not a part of Marine vocabulary. I heard it used on a army base; seems they retreet every night (they play a retreet bugle call over a loud speaker). Once a situation arose in Korea at the Chosin Reservoir where a Marine division was completely surrounded by nine Chinese divisions, due to a complete breakdown by army intelligence. The Marines advanced right back through the enemy divisions, taking out many of them as they went. They dragged along a couple army units, thereby saving them, too.

Rockpile, is a renowned piece of real estate in northwestern Vietnam. It was just a big pile of large rocks that stuck up from the flat plain around it. Because of its location, whoever was "king of the hill" controlled a large area. In the history of the world, a relatively few people have ever laid eyes on it. Seems there ought to be a Rockpile Association, with anyone who has seen the rockpile a member!

RPG, is a rocket propelled grenade. There were generally two types used in Vietnam—a B-40 (RPG-2) and a B-41 (RPG-7).

R&R, rest and relaxation, all servicemen on a one-year tour to Vietnam could take at least one five-day R&R to one of several places around the world.

RTO, a radio telephone operator, or the radioman who is supposed to be school trained and holding the 2531 MOS, but all too often their training was "slim to none," as someone else in the platoon was assigned to carry the radio, or some lieutenant would do the honors himself. "Proper procedures don't necessarily just automatically come with lieutenant's bars, ya know."

Rubber Lady, is the commonly used term for a rubber air mattress, none of which hold air for very long, but they are waterproof. In fact, the term is so common, I was a Marine for quite awhile before I realized that wasn't the correct term for it.

SigInt, signals intelligence—the exploitation of an enemy's signal emissions, which is one aspect of EW, or electronic warfare.

Sit Rep, is a situation report

Skipper, is any Marine C.O., regardless of rank, or the size of the unit that he commands. He can properly and respectfully be called "skipper." It's often a Marine term of endearment, but commonly just respect. To call a Marine "skipper" is kind of a personal thing and definitely not a requirement.

Snake, short for snake-eye, 250 lb, HE bombs

Socked-In, is a term for a very thick cloud cover.

Street Without Joy, was the northernmost section of Highway 1 (the main north-south highway near the coast) that went from Quang Tri north through Dong Ha, and up through the DMZ. The total length was only about 15 to 20 miles long.

TAOR, is tactical area of operational responsibility—the common military terminology for the assigned area of operations for any unit. For instance, the very northern I Corps area was the 3rd Marine Division's TAOR. Farther south by DaNang, Charlie Ridge, the Arizona Territory, the Que Son Mountains, etc., was the TAOR for the 1st MarDiv.

TID, is a "Triple I Device"—imagination, innovation and initiative

Top, is a master sergeant E-8, or sometimes (but not often) used to refer to a master gunnery sergeant E-9. Never is it used to refer to a 1st sergeant, or a sergeant major, at the risk of some terrible adversity befalling the offender. That's almost as bad as a recruit calling a drill instructor, a DI.

Thermite grenade A red grenade shaped like a smoke grenade. Quite heavy, it's not designed for throwing, but primarily for incendiary purposes. It burns very hot and will melt steel quite easily.

Thump gun, was the army's slang name for an M-79

Trolling, is a term for flying low and slow over an area to locate the enemy by getting him to react with movement or fire.

VCB, Vandergrift Combat Base was named for General Alexander A. Vandergrift, the hero of Guadalcanal, who became the Corps' first four-star general in April 1945.

Viet Cong, were the bad guys that weren't North Vietnamese. They generally wore what we would recognize as black pajamas, rather than the uniforms of the NVA. There weren't too many of them left in 69–70 in the northern I Corps area. The only enemy I ever saw there were the NVA, although I believe the army hadn't gotten rid of them all in the other corps areas, and there were still many of them south of DaNang, especially around An Hoa.

Vietnamization is the name of a presidential program begun by Richard Nixon shortly after, becoming president. His idea was to have the South Vietnamese government take a larger part of the military responsibility, eventually allowing the U.S. to completely remove all of its ground forces. In June '69 an announcement was made that 25,000 troops would make up the first increment and in December another 60,000 were to be withdrawn.

Water blivet, is a conical container much like a black balloon, made from some thick black rubber like material.

Water Buffalo, is an oxen-type animal, with large scimitarlike horns. They are prized possessions of a Vietnamese family, and are used for pulling carts, plowing and other mundane chores. They absolutely do not like the smell of Americans.

Water bull, is a large cylindrical container on two wheels that is used to carry water. It is sometimes referred to as a water buffalo.

WIA, wounded in action

Willie Peter Bag, is the common term for a standard issue water proof bag. It also was sometimes called a Wilson Pickett bag, and a couple other names.

Yards, is short for Montagnards, who were a nomadic mountain people and considered to be second-rate citizens. Reportedly, they have been dealt with severely by the Vietnamese government since the communist takeover. America has received them with open arms, and they are now centered in the mountains of North Carolina.

Yard Bracelet, is a silver or brass bracelet worn by most Montagnards, all of which had unique designs. Many Americans traded for them as souvenirs, though some were given as gifts. I sure do wish I had another one!

To Help the Reader Understand

These stories have been written generally in a chronological order and cover a period from August 1969 through August 1970. There are several parenthetical excursions into a previous or a later time, but they help to better explain the proceedings in the stories.

Additionally, the reader will better understand the terminology by making oft reference to the glossary.

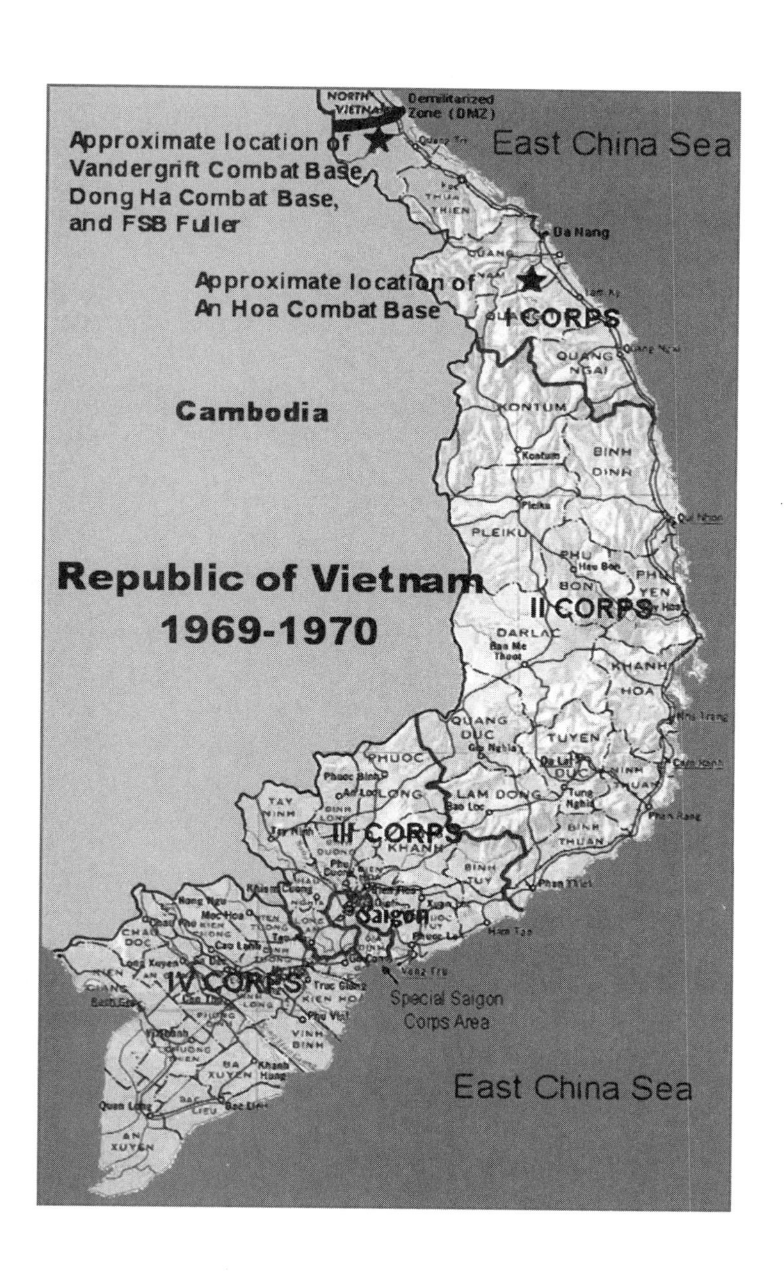
NORTH VIETNAM
Demilitarized Zone (DMZ)
Approximate location of Vandergrift Combat Base, Dong Ha Combat Base, and FSB Fuller
East China Sea
Da Nang
Approximate location of An Hoa Combat Base
I CORPS
QUANG NGAI
Cambodia
KONTUM
BINH DINH
PLEIKU
Republic of Vietnam
1969-1970
II CORPS
DARLAC
KHANH HOA
QUANG DUC
TUYEN DUC
PHUOC LONG
LAM DONG
TAY NINH
III CORPS
BINH THUAN
BINH TUY
Saigon
IV CORPS
Special Saigon Corps Area
East China Sea
AN XUYEN

1 The Stud Scorpion

My arrival in Vietnam was a forgettable experience, therefore I have forgotten most of it. I do recall the "face-off," seeing all those lean and tan Marines as they awaited their turn to board the aircraft from which we had just arrived. I wondered how many were left of their original number, as they watched us NUGs (new guys), knowing that we would be less in number and greatly changed in that eternity of a year before we too would be in their position. Later that evening I was in a transient barracks, and whoosh, BANG!—a rocket attack the very first night. We all ran out quickly into the bunker that was situated right behind the building. I remember thinking, "Is that all there is? Whoop-de-doo!"

"one small step..." and all that jazz.

It was right at the end of July 1969 when I first went to Vietnam. Neil Armstrong had just walked on the moon the 20th of July, 1969 while I was still at Las Pulgas, Camp Pendleton, finishing up "staging." The day after my arrival in DaNang, my new unit, the 1st Radio Battalion (1st RadBn) sent me to VCB (Vandergrift Combat Base) it was also called Stud because before it was a combat base, it was just an LZ named Stud. VCB was in the very north of the "I" Corps area. You see, in 1965, militarily, the country of South Vietnam was divided up into four corps areas, and the 4th or Roman numeral IV was the farthest corps area south (the Mekong River Delta area), while the 1st or "I" corps area was the farthest north, next to the Demilitarized Zone (DMZ or "Z" for short). That's where the Marines were at.

I was riding north from DaNang to Dong Ha in a 6-by with Master Sergeant John Murphy who had been at Company "H" Marine Support Battalion, Homestead, Florida, when I was there several months earlier. Top Murphy was a big guy and had an excellent knowledge of Vietnam's history. The Top told me to polish my boots, giving me a lecture on my unshined boots—in a combat zone. "Come on Top, gimme a break!"

Seems like Captain Eckman was the OIC for the 1st RadBn platoon at Stud. It was interesting, heading up there via 6-by, through the Hai Van pass, and on up past Phu Bai and Quang Tri, then on up the "Street Without Joy" to Dong Ha. From there it was west on Highway 9 past the Vinh Dai Crusher (Sea Bees, 3rd Tank Battalion), past Camp J. J. Carroll, Cam Lo, Khe Gio Bridge, FSB Fuller, the rockpile and on down into VCB. We were "locked and loaded" west of Dong Ha, but only fired on a wild boar, which the whole convoy opened up on.

At VCB, the 1st RadBn area was on the side of a hill to the right just after entering. The Ops (operations) bunker was right next to our living bunker. Someone had made sleeping racks, about two or three high, up against the walls of the bunker. They were like bunk beds, but just plywood, and we slept on "rubber

The Greek, Hawk and Dave at Hill 37. Courtesy of Tim Lundberg

ladies" (inflatable mattresses) with a poncho liner. I can't remember using mosquito nets there, but we sure did later when I was in An Hoa. Regardless, there were a whole bunch of bugs of many different varieties—some recognizable and many that were unknown. I'll never forget the scorpions; there were lots of them. I believe Bob Hrisoulis, the "Greek," arrived there just a few days before I did, maybe a week before, but not much. His magnetic personality and piquant smile caused him to be very much accepted and liked by everyone else. The Greek was like an old hand already, it took me awhile longer. He had the sleeping rack next to mine, but on the bottom. We became fast friends.

One time he started yelling about a bug crawling on him, and then he yelled, "It's a scorpion" as he scrambled to the floor. About that time everyone got into the action—either watching or actively taking part in disposing of the pest. We all were just wearing shorts, because of the heat. Greek started crawling on the floor under the rack among the boots. At the same time one of the other guys started shaking Greek's rubber lady and poncho liner on his rack. About that time, the scorpion fell onto Greek's bare back and he nearly ended his tour right then and there. He wasn't stung, but he sure made a big fuss. I thought we were about to have a fight. The whole bunch of guys thought it was hilarious—that is, everyone but the Greek.

Di Dah, Di Da Dit

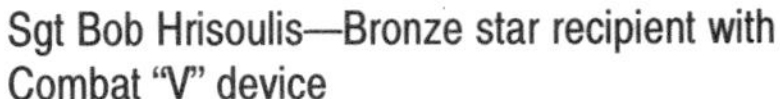

Sgt Bob Hrisoulis—Bronze star recipient with Combat "V" device

2 Beans 'n Balls

THERE ARE TWO MARINE CHOW HALLS THAT WILL ALWAYS HAVE an inexpungible mark in my mind. The first is the Camp Geiger chow hall by Camp Lejeune, North Carolina in 1967; I'll never forget the car tires around the rims of the trash cans for banging the food off the stainless steel trays. Those tires had green stuff growing on them and hanging down off the sides of the tires about an inch or two. Even with all the Marines walking around, working and eating, several rats had grown bold enough to scurry around right there in the open. The second, but most infamous, chow hall to my memory is the 4th Marines chow hall at VCB (Vandergrift Combat Base) "down south" in "Da Nam." (Both of those terms were used to refer to the country of South Vietnam.)

The Rockpile, looking northwest towards the Razorback, and on towards North Vietnam—this is the defining picture

CH-46 Sea Knight with External Load.

It was the first few days of August 1969, and my very first memory of Stud is on the road (Hwy 9) as we were first approaching, having turned south at the rockpile. There were several birds in the air; one was a CH-46 Sea Knight helicopter flying over us on towards Stud just up ahead. The most interesting thing about that bird—and foreboding too—was that it had an external net hanging from underneath. The net was full of dead bodies, with arms and legs hanging out—Marines from the 2nd Battalion, 4th Marine Regiment, or 2/4 Marines.

> *As I approached VCB for the very first time, a Marine CH-46 flew just over us with an external net carrying the bodies of 19 Marines from Echo and Fox Companies, 2nd Battalion, 4th Marine Regiment. They had been in combat with the 304th NVA Division in two battles on Hill 484 which was part of Mutter's Ridge, just north of Dong Ha mountain, and FSB Fuller. Seventy-five Marines were also WIA in that action.*

Shortly after entering the outer perimeter, we made a right, crossed a stream and went up the side of the mountain just a little ways to the 1st Radio Battalion Compound which was to be my home for the next five or six weeks.

For the 1st Rag Bag guy's chow we often had a choice—either C-rations or we had access to the 4th Marine Regimental chow hall. Most of the time we just ate C's though. Periodically, we'd jump into the back of our two-and-a-half ton (deuce and a

Mike Netto, Randy "Fuzzy" Linck w/blooper, Mo Mettinger and Schaffer in the back of the 6-by. Courtesy of Randy Linck

half), which was also called a "multi-fueller," or a "6x6," which was shortened to "6-by." We'd make a little trip down and across the stream, turn south towards the LZ for a little ways, then right back across the stream and up a little bit to the chow hall. Up just a little farther was the battalion aid station (BAS).

My first remembrance of the 4th Marines marvelous chow hall was notable. It was an all-wooden building, painted green of course, with a high roof, unlike any other construction in the area. Upon first entering from the bright light, it seemed dark until the eyes adjusted. It was a smoke-filled room with many little shafts of light streaming in through all the shrapnel holes. Moving in line to get my chow, I got everything I could get as I had a very rapid metabolism and ate like a horse. But, all I could get was a paper napkin (imagine that in Nam, a paper napkin?) and a plastic knife.

There were no paper plates nor other plastic utensils of any kind. The only food was a big piece of meat that the messman, dressed in white, was slicing off for each man as we passed before him. And that was the usual. I never remember one time when we got a complete meal, accouterments and all. It was often just plastic spoons, paper plates and one course of food. I remember once the only thing they had was plastic forks, paper cups and string beans. So, that was the reason the guys just ate C's!

Ah yes, the C's—there's only 12 of them you know, and four of them are inedible, which leaves eight. Now of the different edible C-rations, four of them have to be eaten in bright sunlight so you can see exactly what you're getting. I remember one time, I think it was at Stud, when I was in the darkness of a bunker. Someone—maybe it was Gunny Longstreet—had popped the band on the case of C's (with a twist from a flash suppressor), and hands quickly scarfed up the choice meals. I ended up with spaghetti, not my favorite. After scooping up a big spoonful of spaghetti—or so I thought—I put into my mouth something thick and very slimy. Immediately I gagged, and back out it came. And, then there were seven—edible meals that is—and I'd only been there a couple weeks.

Willard Easley

Some of the stuff we got from the C-rations was amazing; a few of the cases were dated back to the Korean War. I quickly started sticking to beans 'n balls (beans with meatballs in tomato sauce). It was safe—and edible too!

So there it was! Beans 'n balls for breakfast, beans 'n balls for lunch and beans 'n balls for dinner. I became a quick study of the Gunny, and as soon as a case was opened, my hand shot like a flash for those beans 'n balls. Week after week it was beans 'n balls for every meal, unless I messed up. "The early bird gets the worm," you know.

And then it happened! Everything was going along just copasetic for several weeks, maybe six weeks, when I popped open a can of beans 'n balls and it had a bad odor, so I went to something else. Then the next meal/next can of beans 'n balls smelled bad, too, and every single can of beans 'n balls the whole rest of my time down south just about gagged me to smell it. Now, I was down to six edible C-rats, and I still had a lot of time left in-country.

Di Dah, Di Da Dit

3 Boom—Just Like That

The Greek was a little smaller than me, very muscular and well built, and Palmer was a big guy. No, Palmer was a really big guy, and strong. "What was his first name?" At the 1st RadBn compound, in a field of red dirt where the generators were, there at VCB, we had unloaded several 55-gallon drums of diesel fuel from the 6-by to be used by our two 20 KW generators.

Often in the sultry afternoons, we would get those notorious afternoon rains. One day, after a particularly hard afternoon rain, the water was flowing and much of it was in the field around those barrels of fuel. We had to move them under the covering that was made for the generators, our rudimentary generator shack. Our purpose was to set those barrels up, out of the mud, onto some planks. Greek and I were rocking a barrel back and forth to unstick it from the red mud, and we were really struggling with the thing. Palmer came over and flexed his arms, moving the two of us out of his way. Then he gave that barrel a bear hug, picked

Chuck Truitt w/salty boots and cammies at the Hai Van Pass

the whole thing up out the mud, and set it down on the planks. "There, that's how you do it," he said. Seems to me that the Corps should have made him a 81mm mortarman so that he could carry around the baseplate. When our 6-by had a flat, Ol' Palmer would take that tire off the truck, break those split rims and fix the flat in no time at all. That guy could really manhandle a multi-fueller. Come to think of it, I'm glad he was with us and not a mortarman.

Around the last of August 1969, some of those NSA (National Security Agency) guys caused us to be brought up a barrage balloon. The reason was highly classified at the time. We were raising the balloon, which had an antenna box attached for the purpose of receiving a type of radio waves that were traveling along a particular path in the troposphere. Secret stuff. We had a bunch of black bottles of compressed helium gas to keep that balloon filled to the proper pressure. Up and down, up and down, we'd raise it and lower it via the winch on the front of the 6-by. It was a daily occurrence. The whole experiment was unsuccessful and didn't last very long; not like over at 1st RadBn in Dong Ha.

The barrage balloon with antenna box beneath —Courtesy of Gary Williams

NSA's barrage balloon at Dong Ha.
—Courtesy of Rick Swan

I often thought of my initial greeting upon entering VCB; that is, the external net of Marine bodies slung below that CH-46. It always made me more aware of my mortality, and the fact that there were innumerable "bad guys" out there just dying to kill me.

We had a very large amount of concertina (barbed wire) in large coils, all along our outer perimeter. Of course there had to be guards too. That was a never-ending, pain-in-the-neck job to be added to our regular SigInt mission.

I remember one moonlit night, so bright that every object could be plainly seen, though the eerie shadows caused everything to seem alive and moving. There was a noise coming from a couple of trash cans set down next to a blast wall made from dirt-filled ammo boxes. Although I was sure it was a rat, it still needed to be checked out and investigated. I had on my deuce gear, including a bandoleer, and of course my M16 rifle and flack jacket. Man, those plated Marine jackets were uncomfortable and hot, even at 0-dark-30 in the morning when it ought to be nice and cool. I had it on, but it was unzipped in the front so the air could circulate better. As I approached the two cans, I could see that one was about half full of trash and the other was empty. Moving closer, my rifle was instinctively moved from the ready position in front of me to a much lower and casual position. Then I saw a large rat in the bottom of the empty can. It was standing on his hind legs with his fore legs up as if begging, "Please sir, let me out of here." Now you have to understand that everything took place in an instant, as though my mind was watching it all in slow motion.

That rat lunged from the bottom of that empty trash can and slammed into my chest, just below my neck. I'm sure that he was going for a lip-lock on my jugular but all he got was a mouth full of flack jacket. Pushing off, he was gone into the shadows—boom, just like that. I was stunned. If it had been over just an inch or up about two inches, that rat would have got a mouth full of meat—my meat—and I could just imagine the headlines, "Marine Taken Out By Rat."

Multiple exposure of The Wall in Washington D.C.
—Courtesy of Tim Lundberg

A few weeks earlier, the day after arriving in-country, 1st RadBn issued me my deuce gear, three sets of cammies (we called them "You Can't See Me's"), jungle boots ("I Been There Boots") and a chintzy green, two-piece rainsuit. After donning one set of cammies and the boots, all the extra stuff went into my willy peter bag.

In early September, at VCB, a typhoon was upon us and I had the 0-dark-30 watch. Seemed like a good time to break out the rainsuit which was big enough to wear over all my gear. Just after taking charge of my post, I was walking right next to the concertina and the wind caused my rain suit to catch on one of the barbs. Snaaatch, riiipp, swoosh—that rain suit was gone in an instant—and I never had another one the rest of my time "down south." Imagine the headlines, "Marine Blown Away By Big Wind!"

Captain Paul Snearly
—Courtesy of George Carnako

Earlier, probably that day, or just a day or so before, I had gone over to the Battalion Aid Station (BAS) which was just up the hill from the 4th Marines marvelous chow hall. It had been raining a little bit and I was fortunate to be able to ride over in our "deuce and a half," which Palmer was driving; "man, what was his first name?" We forded a small stream that was slightly swollen by the rain from an approaching typhoon. There was a jeep just ahead of us that was slip, sliding in the stream bed, and the guys who had been in it, except the driver, were standing on the bank yelling at the driver and waving us on, "Naw, we don't need no help. We'll get it out in just a minute."

So, we went right up, past the chow hall, and on up to the BAS. I had to go see the dentist for a tooth ache at Battalion Dental which was collocated with the BAS. As I was standing in line waiting to go in, there was a tall, fine-looking Marine standing right behind me not talking. I started a conversation with the guy, but he just answered with a short garbled sentence. Basically I asked him what his problem was. Come to find out he was being treated for a shrapnel wound to his

A Marine CH-46 Sea Knight.

mouth. Outwardly he looked fine, but there was a small, nearly healed wound on the side of his cheek, and he was being treated there at the 4th Marines Dental for the wound to his mouth. That little piece of shrapnel went through his cheek, then hit his teeth and proceeded to do a flamenco dance in his mouth. You couldn't tell from the outside, but when he opened his mouth or talked, it was apparent that young man was changed for life. We lost 58,000 of America's finest, who wouldn't shirk their duties, but a whole lot more were changed for the rest of their lives. As for me, the dentist sent me out to the hospital ship USS Sanctuary via CH-46. It wasn't urgent so it was a few more days yet before I left.

This is three coil Concertina around the perimeter.

On the way back, we were heading down the side of the hill and saw that the stream was really swollen now. There was muddy water flowing completely over that jeep and a whole bunch of guys just standing there waving us on. Ol' Palmer (what's his first name?) just "gunned" our "deuce and a half," and with the downhill momentum, we crossed that swollen stream with nary a problem. Imagine the headlines, "Marine Croaks In Swollen Stream."

In a couple days the "Phoon" was past and I was on a CH-46 "chopping" towards the USS Sanctuary. Just as we cleared the mountains heading east towards our intermediate stop in Quang Tri, I could hear several bangs on the hull of the bird and two shafts of light appeared. As I watched out the big opening in the tail of the "46," I could see a trail of black smoke. The crew chief, who was standing at the side with an M60 M/G looking out, became quite animated and talked a lot into the integral Mic. We continued on towards our destination though, and after just a short ride, we landed safely in Quang Tri where we switched birds and headed on out to the hospital ship. Man, this place could be hazardous to one's health! Once again, I could just picture the headlines, "Marine Bites The Dust Going To The Dentist."

DI DAH, DI DA DIT

USS Sanctuary, Courtesy of Gary D. Waters —from the Internet

4 Greek and the Proboscis Bug

DID YOU EVER NOTICE THE FACT THAT BUGS DO REALLY WELL in warm weather? The month of August, 1969 was a great month for bugs at Vandergrift Combat Base (VCB) there in the Northwest corner of the Republic of Vietnam (RVN or South Vietnam). Practically all of us 1st Radio Battalion Marines (1st RadBn or 1st RagBag) filled sandbags. Palmer (just can't remember his first name), Bob "The Greek" Hrisoulis, and myself were kind of a team; we seemed to work well together. At VCB there

At VCB, 1st RadBn Lieutenants Rhine, Carnako, and Hamm.
—Courtesy of George Carnako

was always a need for more sandbags. That's one thing that there is never enough of in a combat zone, sandbags. We filled sand bags from the ubiquitous supply of empty ones that were always available. Though it was a never ending chore, the motivation factor for more sand bags was high. Day after day in August we filled sandbags, with that red dirt, in that unbelievable heat.

I was more used to the heat than most of those guys, since I grew up in South Florida. Shoot, I had never even seen snow, except at the movies, or on TV. Once a couple years earlier, about November 1967, I had to "police" the outdoor theater at Camp Geiger while I was there for infantry training (ITR). It was about 0700 Saturday morning and several of us were doing a general policing up of the area from the folks who had used the theater the evening before. I yelled out, *"hey you guys, look at this, you gotta see this, somebody threw this cup down and its still got ice in it from last night!"* The rest of those guys thought I was crazy or something, *"Truitt, you're an idiot!"*

Though the heat was certainly nothing new to me, it sure was hot at VCB in August. One day the Skipper (Captain

VCB (LZ Stud) from 1st Rad Bn area. —Courtesy of Howard Brower

The motivation factor was always high to fill sandbags.

Eckman) came out and told us to "knock off filling the sand bags" because the thermometer was reading 127 degrees.

I was exactly 6' tall, and weighed 165 lbs a few weeks earlier when I first arrived "Down South" in "Da Nam." The heat and lack of abundantly fine home-cooked meals (Linda's a great cook) was causing me to lose weight rapidly; by the time I left Vietnam a year later my weight was only 145 lbs. It was all due to a rapid metabolism which caused me to need copious amounts of food to maintain my normal body weight. Back in "The World" (slang for America) I often emphasized to the waitress that she could sacrifice quality for quantity. Now in Vietnam, I'd augment my regular meals, with extra C-ration cans of just about anything that was left over from the other guy's meals. Especially treasured was a Pecan Nut Roll, or a Date Nut Roll. But, I was still losing weight.

At VCB, our operations bunker required electricity so we had two 20kw generators, in the field below, that ran on diesel fuel. The same field where we parked our 6-by, and where we filled our sand bags. With my knack for mechanics, I was a shoe-in for being the "generator guy," (one of my collateral duties). That's alright, I loved it. There was always one cranked up, and making the electrons flow. Every couple days I'd give one of them a PM, and after a couple weeks I trained The Greek on the generator, and he helped me out.

I'll never forget the perpetual smile on the Greek's face, and he had the ability to "clown around" with any and all work. It was his unique ability to make the hardest work into a game, and make it seem like child's play. One evening several of us were sitting in the bunker and playing cards, "Back Alley," which in Vietnam was almost exclusively a Marine card game. The bunker being much cooler than anywhere else (we had a big fan in there to ventilate the thing—remember—we had generators), it was our number one place to relax.

As we played cards, we were being buzzed by a fly. For some reason the fly was very irritating and persistent, more so than

Making Antennas—The Greek at Hill 37—always the clown. —Courtesy of Tim Lundberg

normal. We were sitting around in shorts, or cutoff cammies, and that fly suddenly landed on Greek's leg just above his knee. Since about six of us were sitting there in a circle, we all saw the fly light on Greek's leg at about the same time.

All of a sudden, zoom, zap, then a pronounced ***"yeow"*** came from The Greek. We were all transfixed by the strangest bug I've ever seen in my life. A large, spindly bug with big translucent wings, and a long proboscis swooped down and impaled that fly on Greek's leg. The bug's nose went all the way through the fly and stuck into Greek's leg. We all gazed in amazement as the big bug fluttered, and then took off with the fly shish-ka-bob on its nose.

"Wow, can you believe THAT?" was on everybody's lips. I don't remember what The Greek said, but you can be sure that it was a winner. And, you can be sure that The Greek told that story over, and over again. (It's absolutely true, guys. I saw it too.)

Greek and I became good friends. He had been raised Greek Orthodox, but it was all just a formality with him. Though he

Greek, making work light at Hill 37. —Courtesy of Tim Lundberg

Chuck Truitt after a bit of a weight loss; notice the "Yard" Bracelet.

called himself a Christian, Bob didn't seem to have any kind of personal relationship with Christ. I believe he had been influenced by the kind of people that the Bible talks about in 2 Timothy 3:5 *Having a form of Godliness, but denying the power thereof....*

Me, I wasn't raised in any particular religion, but I had gone to a church there in Ft. Lauderdale, where I grew up, because of the good looking girls that were there. Once, when I was about thirteen, there was an evangelist who preached the Gospel and I received Jesus Christ as my Savior because I knew that I was a sinner. I definitely didn't want to pay for those sins myself; that would be Hell. I prayed to Jesus and asked him to forgive me, and come into my heart, because I believed that He paid for my sins Himself. Romans 10:8-10 *8 But what saith it? The word is nigh thee, even in thy mouth, and in thy heart: that is, the word of faith, which we preach; 9 That if thou shalt confess with thy mouth the Lord Jesus, and shalt believe in thine heart that God hath raised him from the dead, thou shalt be saved. 10 For with the heart man believeth unto righteousness; and with the mouth confession is made unto salvation.*

It's not that Christ got caught and was executed. He allowed Himself to be crucified and paid for my sins with his own bloody death. He bled to death you know; he died just like the sacrificial lambs under the knives of the priests.

That changed my life. I have never been the same since that time when I was thirteen years old. There have been a lot of times that I didn't act like I was different, but for sure, I've never been the same. I was changed!

Something that I've deeply regretted ever since, is the fact that I never, not even once, told The Greek about the difference trusting in Christ made in my life. It is more than just a formal religious thing; it is a personal relationship. Christ shed His blood for me personally, and I wasn't bold enough to even tell my friend.

Greek and I were split up after we left VCB, but we maintained contact. When I got my orders for Company "B" in Scotland I gladly received them, and took my wife and baby daughter. I was tempted a little to extend for another six months in Nam; the Greek did, but I took my orders and "didi maued" out of there.

After my last letter to The Greek in the Fall of '70, I didn't hear from him for awhile. Then sometime around the end of February 1971 I received a letter, there in Scotland, from Dave McWatters (Greek's Platoon Commander) telling me that Bob "The Greek" Hrisoulis was KIA on the 21st of January 1970.

No, I never told Bob about trusting in Christ, and the change it would make in his life. But, I do know that if he did, at sometime, receive Christ as his Savior, that I'll see my friend, and his electric smile again one day. It will always be on my heart and mind that I never told him when I had the chance, while he was still alive. By-the-way, I've learned to be much more bold today, and I try to tell the Gospel as often as I can.

I'll say, "*Hey Greek! Remember the time we were playing Back Alley, and that big Proboscis Bug zapped your leg?*" Ha!

(This particular story was awhile writing. I'm very sad that I let my friends down. Both of my friends, Jesus Christ, and The Greek.)

Di Dah, Di Da Dit

This is the last known photograph of the Greek just a couple days before being KIA, 21 Jan 71. —Courtesy of Randy Linck

5 My Own Private Air Taxi

After spending about five or six weeks at Vandergrift Combat Base (LZ Stud), which was nestled between some lush, verdant mountains, our 1st Radio Battalion unit pulled back to Dong Ha, nearer the coast. Stud was a little southwest of the Rockpile in the very northwest corner of RVN (Republic of VietNam). I was a Marine Corporal and the date would have been several days into September 1969.

Actually, I had been a corporal since back when I was promoted at Company "H," Marine Support Battalion, Homestead Air Force Base, way in the south of Florida. I'll never forget when I went up before the promotion board in November 1968, because our 50 man Marine unit was attached to a Navy unit there on that Air Force base, which was a rather unique situation. There was a Navy Lt. Cmdr. amongst the Marines on my meritorious promotion board. The board asked me a bunch of questions such as, "what's your 5th General Order?, what's the bias on your trouser leg?, and what does the names Maddox, and Turner Joy mean to you?" That squid (Navy person) asked me one question only, "how do you like working with the Navy?" Now Gunny Weeks had just coached me before going into the promotion board, *Truitt, the best thing you can do is answer those questions honestly, and to the best of your ability; don't try and "blow any smoke."* As a result of his coaching, my answer to that Lt. Cmdr. was as honest as I could make it. Well, I got the meritorious promotion, but the Gunny told me, *Truitt, that was poor judgment: "Sir, if I had'a wanted to work with the Navy, I'd a joined the Navy!" was not the right answer. You'd of been promoted as of 1 December, but now it won't be till 1 January 1969.* Ha! So much for honesty—you don't get points for honesty—when you're a Marine working with the Navy. (Man, come to think of it, I've got a couple good stories from Company "H," but later!)

Back at Vandergrift, a typhoon had just passed by thoroughly soaking and blowing things about, there in the first few days of September '69. I can remember absolutely nothing about the move from Vandergrift Combat Base; just all of a sudden we were back in Dong Ha.

Within a few days after arriving in Dong Ha, SSgt Dave Carpenter, who was the guy in charge of keeping the HFDF (high frequency radio direction finding) nets up and operable, came to me. Dave said, *"Truitt, I understand that you want to work DF. Get your stuff together because we need you to go to the LZ and catch a bird up to Dong Ha mountain"* (FSB Fuller). Before driving me over to the LZ, Dave took me out to the "Pig Pen" and gave me a crash course on operating the PRD-1 radio direction finder, which we called a Pig. (Of course I already had the prime prerequisite, a knowledge of Morse Code.) Dave also showed me the finer details of using the Comus pad, a thick booklet with many pages from which we could encrypt all the pertinent information necessary to do our job.

SSgt Dave Carpenter—Courtesy of Al Kruger

First stop was the LZ at Dong Ha where I told them "Dong Ha Mountain." The wait there wasn't too long, maybe an hour or two, and the guy in the control shack said *"Truitt there's a bird gonna drop in, and pick you up to take you on up to Fuller."*

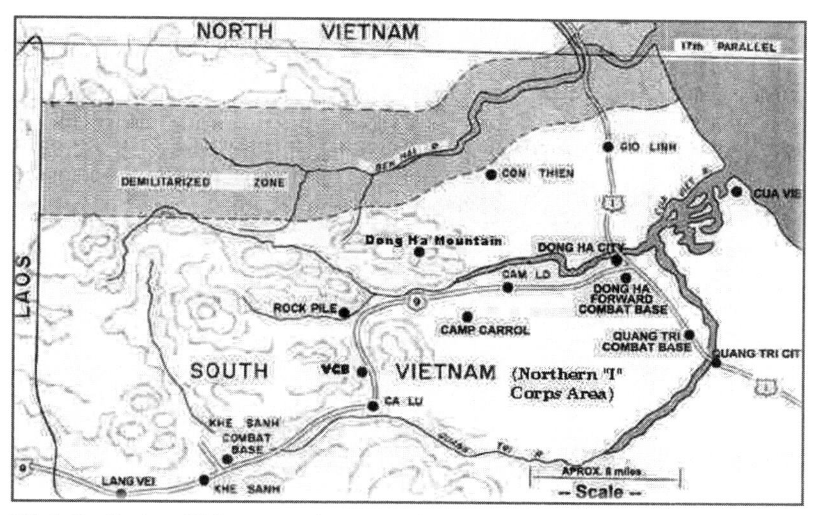

This is the Northern "I" Corps area, just south of the DMZ.

Hot Dog! I was definitely ready, and all my stuff was ready to go too. Dave had driven me over in a jeep with my Willie Peter bag (water proof bag) of personal gear, a whole grunch of batteries, two cases of Black Label beer, a U.S. Mail bag with mail for the 1st RadBn guys, and my "deuce gear" (short for Form 782 Issue, or combat gear). The bird that dropped in was a LOaCH (Light Observation CHopper) also called a "BB" which is a Hughes-500, the same kind of bird that "TC" flew on the TV program "Magnum PI" except the tail was a little different. There were only two men aboard, the pilot and the observer; they stopped just for me! Wow, my own private "air taxi."

The flight from Dong Ha up to the mountain was not long, as I believe it was probably 10-15 miles WNW of the Combat Base, and just a very few thousand meters from the DMZ with the Song Bin Hai (river) running down the center of the "Z." There were birds flying around up in that area all the time, but when one landed at Fuller, it was always greeted by smiles from everyone up there. There were probably 200 to 250 men at any given time. There would have been about 150-175 men in the

This is a LOaCH from 240th Assault Helicopter Company.

infantry company, and possibly 75-100 arty boys for the six 105's and associated arty stuff, plus the 5 or 6 of us 1st Rad Bn guys.

Whenever a bird landed there was usually a bunch of guys heading to the pilot or crew to hand them letters to mail (no stamps required). I always wrote in the stamp area "Fly it, it's Free." Sometimes I handed them a film cannister to be developed along w/some MPC (money—Military Payment Certificates). Those guys always took care of us too. Next flight out they would have the developed film, or the transistor radio that I requested, or whatever within reason.

Those pilots and air crew were really decent folks, to a man! I watched a few of them die from up there too. For instance I saw two Cobras go down within a few minutes of each other, another time I saw a CH-46 go down. I'll never forget the F4 Phantom on a bombing run a few weeks later, sometime in October it seems, which flew right straight into the deck. There were two Phantoms making bombing runs on a ridge line just NW of us. They were flying in a big circle 180 degrees apart, and as each approached the target in a dive, they'd flip over on their back to spot the target, then flip back over and release some bombs, after which they'd shoot back up to altitude to get in the big circle and make another run while the other Phantom did his thing. One of the Phantoms flipped over to see the target, I heard a 51 Cal. ChiCom M/G chattering, and the jet never flipped back over, but just flew inverted into the deck.

When we set down on the LZ there was a bunch of guys there, all hunkered down, or holding on to engineer's stakes, or something to keep from blowing over the side in the choppers wash. My guys were there to help with the beer, batteries and supplies, and to show me where to go. Since the LZ was just north of the center of the 150 yard long by about 30 to 40 yard wide crest, even the farthest extremity wasn't very far. Our 1st RadBn Ops (Operations) bunker was just north of the LZ and on

20mm cannon fire from an F4 on an enemy force on the ridge line just north of us.

Dong Ha mountain / FSB Fuller.—Courtesy of George Carnako

the western side. For the first couple days I bunked with some grunts from 2/4 in a bunker next to the LZ, that is, until we dug out an 81mm ammo storage area next to the Ops bunker. Prior to my arrival, I guess they were all "hot racking it" in one section of the Ops bunker. As I unloaded, I was introduced to the guys. *"This here's SSgt. Chuck Colvard, and that's Sgt. Tom Cunningham, and there's Cpl. Bill Morris—you'll be working with him on the Pig for awhile—and this guy here's Howie "orange socks" Spaulding, from Las Vegas* (I'm thinking, what, is this guy nuts or something? Orange Socks?) Yepper, he's nuts alright! *And, Ol' Milford Cole, from Sugartown, LA*"—a real basketball player—I knew Cole from Company "H." Man, what a crew! *"Truitt, you aint sleeping in here with us!"* I guess I smelled too sweet, Ha! You know what? Those guys really were some of America's finest young men. I'm proud to have associated with them, and with the United States Marine Corps. They weren't like so many back in the States who were only wrapped up in themselves and/or wasting their lives with drugs and stuff. A large number of Americans were rationalizing, or coming up with some excuse to keep from serving our great country.

For awhile, till after SSgt Joe Armstrong replaced SSgt Chuck Colvard, the entrance to the Ops bunker faced west with a sand-bagged wall blocking so that the "little people" couldn't shoot straight inside from the next ridge over. But, there was just a 6 or 7 foot wide ledge along the front of the entrance with a drop past the ledge of about 8 to 10 feet. That's where a whole bunch of extra coiled concertina, razor wire was stored. There was a bunch of it, and if you fell off the ledge, you were in "deep kimchee." Come to find out, that's why I had to make a quick arrival at Fuller. The guy that I was replacing had unfortunately rearranged his facial features and body characteristics just a couple days earlier when he made a head long plunge off the ledge into the wire. It was also his RTD (rotation date), and I'm sure that he was ready to leave Vietnam. And, now it was my turn at Fuller to work HFDF.

DI DAH, DI DA DIT

SSgt Joe Armstrong at the Hai Van pass.

6 Well Twang My Twanger

THE ANIMALS AND INSECTS ARE SOME OF THOSE THINGS THAT I believe are suitable, interesting to recall, and relate stories of concerning Vietnam. And, of course the Rats.

Marine CH-53A carrying BBs. Courtesy of Randy Linck

In South Vietnam, at the top of Dong Ha mountain (Fire Support Base, Fuller) about the end of September 1969, we had a rat problem. Let me tell you a bit about FSB Fuller first though. Fuller, from what I was told, had been taken from the NVA several times over the past few years, but then it was abandoned to other operations elsewhere. Every time though, the NVA went back and used the commanding heights to watch American forces in the whole area. After fighting for Dong Ha mountain for the third time we got smart, and kept it manned. One could clearly see the large red flag with the yellow star flying in the DMZ just a couple thousand meters to the north. Also, we could easily see other places too, like Con Tien- NNE, Gio Lin- east, Dong Ha- southeast, and Camp Carroll- SSE. Looking further around to the SSW we could see The Rockpile, and on past towards the Khe Sanh valley. To the west was the Razorback, and further still, Laos. It was an absolutely beautiful sight, especially when the sun was rising and there was a blanket of clouds rolling down the valleys.

Sgt Rick Swan with a PRD-1 at Dong Ha, before completion of the Pig Pen. Notice the dirt filled ammo boxes.

Not only was it good for observation, but we put 105mm howitzers up there to provide fire support for ongoing operations. Of course, we had several 81mm mortars, recoilless rifles

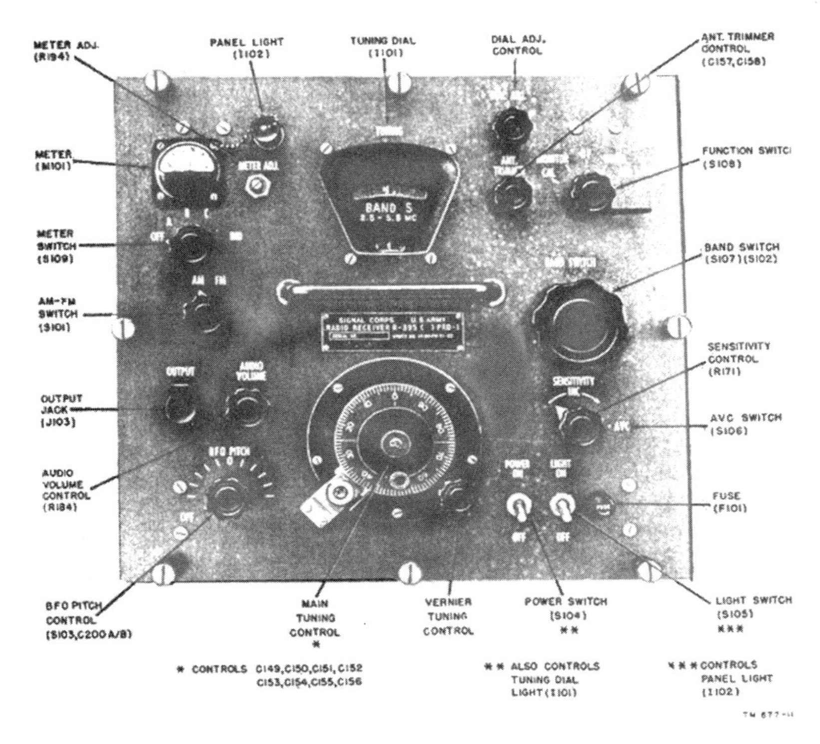

Figure 11. Radio Receiver R-395/PRD-1, front panel.

a PRD-1, "PIG"

and "beau coup" other smaller weapons too. Me, I had a rifle and an M-79 grenade launcher, "blooper" (the army called them "thump guns"). I used the blooper for H&I fires, and fired about a case every seven to ten days, that's a half gross, or 72 HE rounds (which I kept in my bunker, next to my cot). I also fired flares, shotgun rounds—00 Buck, and I fired one CS round. My main weapon though was a pig, which had been used in WW II, so I was told. A pig was a PRD-1 which stands for "portable, radio, direction, series 1." Mine was serial number 0014. My pig had shrapnel holes in the top, but it worked just fine. With it I could shoot an azimuth on an enemy radio transmission. If three or more guys could get a shot on a radio in transmission, depending on the situation, we could call fire on the enemy location using big guns, little guns or air strikes. Or we could call in a ground unit as well. My pig and I really helped to make a lot of VC and NVA unhappy.

When I first arrived at Fuller, I slept in a bunker about ten yards from our operations bunker on a piece of plywood. At least it was off the ground, but it was absolutely pitch black inside except for a flashlight or the usual smoky, 81mm mortar, twisted wax candle. However, the guys from my small detachment needed a different sleeping area, rather than with the bi-weekly rotating grunt companies. We chose a lean-to type bunker that stored several hundred 81mm mortar rounds, but it had to be dug out so we could stand up inside. Of benefit was that it was right next to the Ops bunker, and if I recall, the pig pen where I had my PRD-1 was right up on top. After we dug it out, the walls all the way around were just dirt and clay, measuring about seven feet by nine feet. PSP (steel runway matting) formed the ceiling, and it was all covered with about three rows of sandbags.

Back to the rat problem. Shortly after completing the digging and moving in, rat holes appeared all around the inside. It

Dong Ha Mountain from the East, Cam Lo, on the edge of Leatherneck Square.

was the beginning of monsoon season, with lots of fine misty rain at that 549-meter altitude. Since water leaked onto my cot, I hung plastic sheeting at the head, a few inches from the dirt wall, to just past the foot of my cot, and about three feet above. That way I could sit erect comfortably. At the foot, the plastic was more loose so that when the water dripped down from the roof to the plastic, it would run on down and drip off the end, rather than pool up and eventually collapse due to the weight of the water.

One night I awoke to some strange seesawing noise. I looked with my flashlight, and there straight up was a fair-sized rat that had dug a hole out of the wall where the plastic ended over the head of the cot. Right there in the dirt wall, just over my head, was a newly dug hole. The rat was merrily swinging with his two hind feet on the edge of the hole and his two front feet on the plastic. Instantly, after I shone my light on the rat, he pushed off

Looking SSW from FSB Fuller, with the rockpile on past in the valley.

with his hind feet and slid down the plastic, like a sliding board right off the bottom end. He fell to the floor at the foot of my cot, then ran on out of the bunker at the entrance, right there by my feet. Well, that really "twanged my twanger," and my anger too. It was right then that I determined to eradicate the rats, and since we had no rat traps up there, it would take every bit of my inventive genius. Furthermore, regular rat traps weren't large enough for those big boys. As a result, we shot them, stuck them, blew them up, killed them with pitfalls and got them with other devices too.

DI DAH, DI DA DIT

7 Whoosh, Pop: Mad Minute

I HAD ONLY BEEN ON DONG HA MOUNTAIN FOR JUST A LITTLE while before they gave me the lowdown on our defensive fires and procedures. We had an area of the perimeter to defend that

FSB Fuller from our defensive portion of the wall, looking down the west side towards the ravine

was adjacent to our operations bunker on the NW side of the mountaintop. Our assigned defensive area was only a few yards long, and it was just a little past the bend in the wall on our left.

It was there that the side of the mountain fell away at about a 45-degree angle, and we had maybe 60 or 70 yards cleared out for a clean field of fire. A ravine was on past our cleared area. There were, if I recall properly, about three strands of coiled French concertina razor wire, plus several other strands of just plain old barbed wire. The whole area had numerous cans in the wire to detect any movement, and it was booby trapped with illumination flares, foo gas barrels and claymore mines. Foo gas was nasty stuff—a mixture of napalm, diesel fuel and some kind of detergent to help it stick to whatever it landed on, rather than just run off like a liquid. The foo gas was mixed and poured into some kind of container—usually a drum or artillery round tube container—which was usually at least half buried and sandbagged behind it (towards us) so that when it was detonated, it would blow out towards the bad guys. Most of the time the foo gas was blown with a charge of C4, using an electrical blasting cap and a clacker (squeeze detonator).

My first "mad minute" brought a slight amount of trepidation, as I didn't know quite what to expect. I kind of had images of "little people" coming at us en masse through the coils of concertina razor wire. Actually, the officer in charge would call for the mad minute if something suspect was happening outside our perimeter. The word was passed and everyone would go on the firing line in their defensive positions. So the whole mountaintop perimeter was heavily manned within just a couple minutes. Everyone had their overlapping fields of fire covered. All of a sudden a pop-up hand flare would go "whoosh, pop" and the brightness of the flare would burn for about 40 to 45 seconds. During that time everyone would open up with everything they had. It was actually just short of a minute of final protective fire.

The noise and din of a mad minute was unbelievable. I could usually empty four full magazines of 18 rounds, and be ready to go with one more by the time the flare flickered and extinguished. Personally, I didn't like to put tracers in my rifle magazines but some of the guys did, which only added to the spectacle. It was always an extremely exciting time with a huge adrenaline rush. I understand that the 105mm howitzers had flechette (little nails with fins) canisters ready to be loaded and fired over the edge by lifting up the back of the gun, although I never witnessed that event. Seems to me that the gun would have gone flying off the other side of the mountain—they weren't recoilless rifles, you know!

A few times, rather than my M-16, I'd take my M-79 (blooper) on the line and pop as many HE (high explosive) rounds as I could in that short minute, but most of the time I'd just use the blooper for "H & I" because we could do that at any time after dark. It broke open just like a single-shot shotgun by using a little lever on the back of the gun. When a 40mm round was inserted into the chamber, you'd just close it and fire. Most anyone could fire three before the first one exploded by firing up at a 60 or 70 degree angle and letting the round fall into the ravine to our front. But, by being very familiar with the operation a person could usually get four rounds out before the first one exploded. On two occasions, after setting the rounds along in a line on the sandbagged wall and working the mechanism

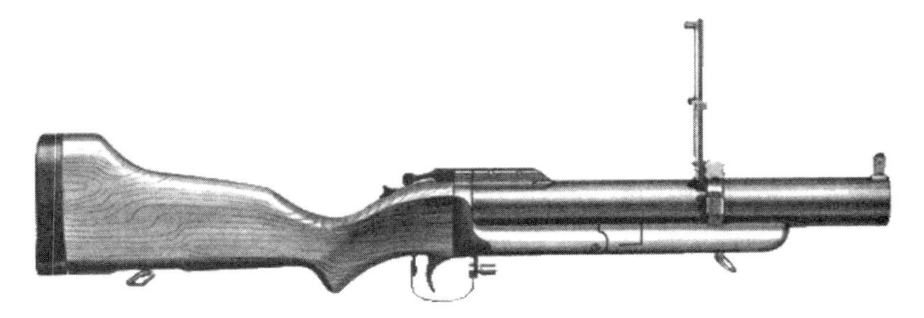

M-79, "Blooper"

really fast there in the dark, I was able to get the last of five squeezed off before the first detonation. The blooper wasn't really suitable for mad minutes though, because the object was to cover your own designated field of fire as thoroughly as possible in that short time span.

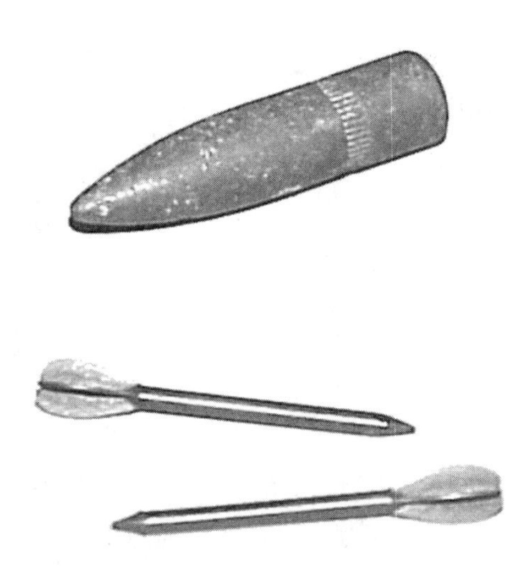

Two flechette with a 30 caliber bullet in comparison.

As soon as the flare extinguished, there was total silence on the whole FSB (fire support base), as everyone listened intently. Periodically, after an instant of listening, someone would open up on a perceived sound, but almost always there was nothing but dead silence. Any enemy probes or reconnoitering had been quashed.

Once a mad minute was called because of some noise in the trash pile a couple hundred feet down on the left of our position, near the salient that extended over towards the other ridge. That was where the bend in the mountaintop formed an elbow, and where the trash chute was located. Whoosh, pop went the flare, and everyone opened up in their own field of fire, but then we immediately saw movement down to our left. It was a big cat of some kind that went bounding in huge leaps, towards the protection of the ravine. Immediately, a couple score of guns shifted fire towards the cat and the ground erupted behind it, but I never saw any indication of anybody actually hitting the thing.

The next day a patrol that covered that section of the perimeter and beyond happened to find the body and brought it back up. The carcass was displayed for all to see there by the LZ.

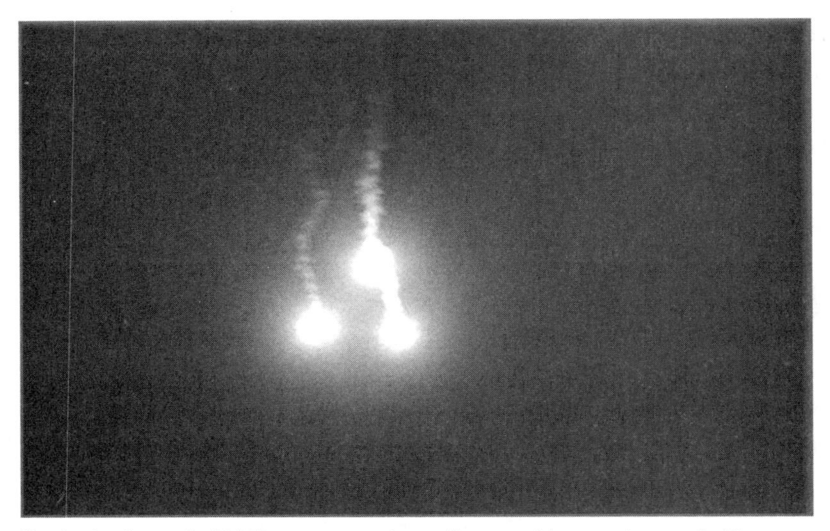

Illumination flares of which there are many types; these are 81mm mortar rounds. The largest are in barrels dropped from aircraft, the smallest are from pop-ups.

I have no idea what kind of cat it was, though it was fairly big, maybe 60 or 70 pounds. He sure had been a pretty thing before carelessly making noise in his reconnoiter of our trash area. What he lacked in stealth, he made up for in beauty. I guess it was "The Cat From Hanoi."

DI DAH, DI DA DIT

8 Pointy End First

WE HAD AN INTERESTING BUNCH OF MARINES ATOP DONG Ha mountain at FSB Fuller around the end of September 1969. Actually in about a three-month period that fall, some of the guys I remember being with us at one time or another were Joe Armstrong, Chuck Colvard, Howie Spaulding, Milford Cole,

Ops Bunker at FSB Fuller about September 1969—Clockwise from left: Spaulding, Cole, Morris, Quan, half of Colvard, Cunningham and Noi.

Tom Cunningham, Bill Morris, Dave Carpenter and a couple ARVN "dancers." Not long after digging out our little sleeping bunker, which had previously stored 81mm mortar rounds, we moved in, along with our ever-present companions, the rats. I swear they followed us everywhere. Even when we went outside the concertina razor wire to patrol the perimeter or to clear brush or blow trees to expand our fields of fire, we could hear their movement and scurrying; at least I believe that's what it was most of the time—NVA Rats.

My little sleeping bunker was just big enough for a max of four cots, but we usually had two or three. Three sides of the bunker were just dirt, and the front, facing west, was made from sandbags with an opening at the south end of the sandbags. My cot lay along the sandbagged wall with the foot of the cot at the entrance, although a couple weeks later I started sleeping with my head at the entrance, so I could look directly out. That's when I killed the biggest centipede I've ever seen anywhere. It was maybe eight to ten inches long.

Looking west while standing on the LZ, with clouds blanketing the valleys in the early morning. Sometimes that ragged ridge—the Razorback—would be streaked red by the rising sun.

FSB Fuller looking north from the LZ; that's the 1st RadBn bunker just up from the First Aid bunker with the Red Cross. —Courtesy of Joe Armstrong

At Fuller I always slept with my big Buck knife in the cot, as well as my 45. Just at dawn, as the red streaks gave the Razorback ridge to the west a red tint, I would wake in the cool mist of the early morning and watch out the bunker's entrance by my head. It was absolutely gorgeous there and I'll never forget the beauty and serenity of those mornings, not in a thousand years. It was quite the contrast to the hate and discontent that would blossom throughout the northern "I" Corps area in just a little while.

The edge of the sandbags and the entrance was right next to my head. Right there, at eye level, came crawling the head and first couple sections of a huge centipede. It was one of those deep purple-and-blue-hued buggers that you'd see every once in a while. He was right next to my face, just a few inches away. I watched him for a few seconds and he kept coming, and kept coming, on around the sandbag. He was going to come inside and cuddle up in one of our boots under the cots, or worse, maybe even get into the warmth of a cot with the rubber lady, poncho liner, Marine and all. Well, before he was all the way around, I let him have it with my big Buck knife, and in an instant there were two pieces of purple centipede squirming on the dirt floor at the foot of my cot. Then there were three pieces, and then four, etc. "Them are juicy ones too."

The rat problem got so bad that the current company commander (usually a company from 2/4 Marines) passed the word that each morning there would be a rat body count, and the Marine who had the highest body count at the end of the week would get a free five-day in-country R&R. Now I'm not sure that my guys from 1st Radio Battalion would be able to take advantage of a win or not, but we enthusiastically joined the fight. There was a catch though. I don't recall there being any suitable rat traps on

FSB Fuller above the clouds; Major Jim Hatch looking west. Just behind him is the entrance to our sleeping bunker, a dugout 81mm mortar storage bunker. —Courtesy of George Carnako

Fuller, and as a result the top of that mountain became a free-fire zone for rats. You have to understand that I'm not referring to the standard stateside variety of rat; I'm talking about those big boys that wouldn't think twice about confronting you for a pork slice from a C-ration can. I'm convinced that most Americans don't comprehend the size of those things. It was different in Nam, "big rats and little people." We came up with some really interesting methods for upping the body count.

Before I switched to sleeping with my head at the entrance of our little bunker, I slept with my head nearest the dirt wall, with the sandbagged wall at my right hand, and the entrance at my right foot. Across from my foot was the first dirt wall, which was just a couple feet thick and shared with our operations bunker. At the bottom of the dirt wall next to the dirt floor, and about two feet inside the open bunker entrance, was a hole. It was evidently our bunker's main entrance to the "rat estate" from which most of the other rat holes emanated, in both our bunker and the Ops bunker. In fact, it wouldn't have surprised me to find out that it had tunnel connections all the way to Hanoi. (If there was ever such a thing as evolution, I'm sure that the Vietnamese people must have come from the rat line, which would explain their impressive system of tunnels.)

That rat hole was the object of most of our attention. Because it was the wall separating our bunkers, shooting my 45 in that direction was out of the question, but I could—and did—successfully use several other means on that hole. I found that I could, after a little practice, throw my knife from the prone position in my cot, and after half a flip, have it hit the dirt and slide "pointy end first" right into that rat hole. I know for sure that I added to the body count with two KIA, NVA rats. Furthermore, there were at least a couple WIA rats because there was blood on my knife.

Di Dah, Di Da Dit

9 The Squeeze

On top of Dong Ha mountain, FSB Fuller in the fall of 1969 I think that some of those guys from the "Grunt" Company of 2/4 were cheating! I don't know how, but they just had to be cheating because their rat body-count was growing rapidly, faster than mine. I'm sure some of them must have been pooling their kills. I had shot two with my 45 (man, that makes a mess, but not as much as the story I'm about to relate) but I had missed a couple times. Unfortunately, I had put a bit of a ding in the leg of one of the cots. It's hard to aim well enough to hit a rat in subdued light, and we had to have the light low to get those NVA rats to come out far enough to see them, usually. I say usually, because sometimes they'd appear right there—nearby—when you least expected it and weren't ready. By the time you get your 45, and chamber a round—well, "no workie" if you know what I mean.

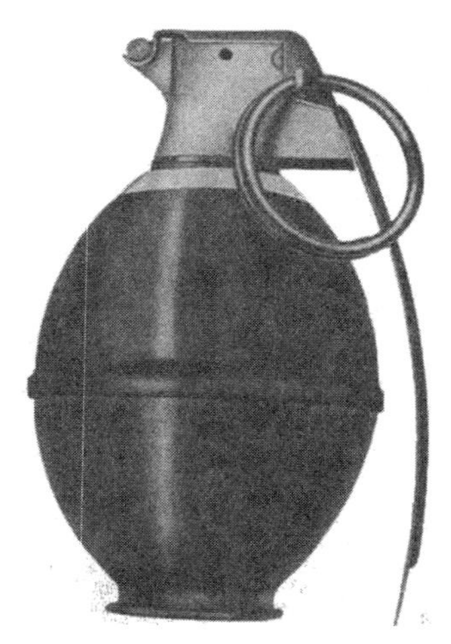

M-26 Fragmentation Grenade

Well, we had been fooling around with an M-26 grenade. I had field stripped the thing and popped the cap on it, which "twanged my twanger" into thinking about increasing my NVA rat body-count (now Joe Armstrong, don't go getting ballistic on me here again!).

"Fighting Joe Armstrong" Hey Joe, where was I when you all had this chow? Uh, oh! BBQ rat? —Courtesy of SgtMaj Joe Armstrong

I got a bunch of electrical blasting caps, the kind that we used with the claymore mines, and a little hand squeeze detonator, which was commonly called a "clacker." After pulling the cots away from the dirt wall, I proceeded to put a cap in each rat hole and run a wire to my rack. After completing that part of the FireEx, I donned my flack jacket and helmet, lit an 81mm mortar, twisted wax candle to give some light—but not too much, then sat quietly waiting. My idea was to insert the proper wire into the clacker when a rat appeared, and squeeze that thing. The problem was, those NVA rats were slick. They didn't appear and look out of the hole to check if it was all clear, then come on out. That's what I was hoping for, and expecting. Nope! It was whoosh, those rats were already moving by the time I could see them.

Over a period of a couple days, the only thing I was doing was scaring little rat poopies out of them, enlarging the holes in

Looking NNW from our Ops bunker. Notice the 105mm shell casing covering the sharp engineer stakes before the army painted them all.

the dirt wall and getting dirt all over the guys' cots. I did manage to make a real mess of one rat who must have had a brain seizure when he saw me, because he made the fatal mistake of going back into his hole just as I gave "the squeeze." Whammo, and then a big gob of rat guts, fur and a leg went splat on top of the guy's cot next to me. (Did you ever stop to consider how long rat intestines are?) I quickly got rid of the mess and I'm sure that Marine (I'll not tell you who it was) never had any idea what happened for several reasons. First off, it was just a blood stain on the poncho liner which quickly dried, and it was dark in there anyhow. Secondly, the other guys were over in the Ops bunker doing the SigInt thing, or playing back ally, or spades or something; I was the only one who saw the results/mess. Thirdly, everything was filthy. (The only water we ever had up there was heli-lifted to us in a water blivet, or in a water bull (there's a great story here) so we never washed our gear, and very rarely ourselves. I got a shower two-and-a-half times (another story) in the over three months I was at Fuller, and both of those times were on resupply runs to Dong Ha. One of those times the water heater caught fire while I was in the shower (I'll let one of you other guys from Dong Ha, who remembers it better than I, relate that story).

This is a clacker to detonate a claymore mine. Attach the wire in the end, duck and squeeze!

Those grunts wouldn't count my rat in the body count because it wasn't all there. They said "someone else might turn in the rest of the rat and it'd get counted twice." Oh yeah? Right! Well, I had gotten another rat nevertheless. But I stopped trying to blow up the rats because it wasn't all that productive and it was really messy. Plus, they didn't count the rat and I didn't want to waste a good kill for nothing.

Di Dah, Di Da Dit

10 Trioxane Trixie

We had a dog on FSB Fuller in the fall of 1969. A typical yellow Vietnamese pooch, this one was adopted by our 1st Radio Battalion folks. The dog was just a few months old when I arrived, and was either born up there or taken up there when very young. The whole fire support base was only about 150 meters long and 50 meters wide. It looked like a boomerang with the longest portion running north to south, and the other section trailing off towards the southwest which was probably about 50 meters lower than the northern end. We had a four foot sandbagged wall all the way around, which was interspersed with many fighting positions and machine gun bunkers. The LZ was about 65 or 70 meters from the north end, and it took up the greater part of the width of the fire support base. The 105s were along the southern arm, and our location was near the top on the west side, which was also where we were responsible for defending about a 60-foot section. We had it all thoroughly covered with overlapping fields of fire. Just to the left, or south, of our part of the wall, was a "four holer" and to the

Trioxane Trixie

right was a machine-gun position that was manned by the Grunt Company. The whole world for our dog was within the perimeter of that FSB, except for periodically when we'd have reason to go over the wall and outside of the concertina wire. I can't remember if that dog's name was Sin or Ox. We had another dog down at Hill 65 and I can't remember which was named which; I'm just going to call this dog Trioxane Trixie.

"Blondie" A typical adult Vietnamese dog.

The only food we had when the Marines were up there was C-rations, some LRPs (long range rations) and PIRs (provisional indigenous rations). I liked the PIRs best, but you had to mix water with them and let them sit for about five to ten minutes before they could be eaten. After the doggies replaced the Marines, which seems like the first or second week of November (wow, what a story), it was kind of scary for a little while. The only Marines left up there were the five of us 1st Radio Battalion guys. One thing about it though, if we weren't socked in (common at that time of year—monsoons, you know), they were faithful to fly in hot chow from some chow hall someplace around Quang Tri.

A Marine Ch-46 Sea Knight approaching the LZ.

Their First Sergeant would usually let us Marines partake of the fresh hot chow, if we were good boys and they had enough. One

Operation Durham Peak, 106mm recoilless rifles. Courtesy of Rob Charnell

time I was a "very bad boy" in their eyes and they cut us all off from the hot chow for awhile. I guess if we'd been on a ship they'd have put us on bread and water, although we still had the C-rats. Well, before we started getting the good stuff from the doggies, our menu was usually C-rats and we heated them with heat tablets (trioxane). Now let me tell you, those things had to be used only with proper ventilation, or we'd get gassed out. We had a particular descriptive word for it, *x*x*x. I'm sure that if we had an artillery attack at the same time as a *x*x*x, every single one of us would choose to leave the bunker and take our chances with the "incoming."

Of note, we didn't always have heat tabs to heat our C-rats, but we always had C-4 explosive. Often we used that rather than the heat tabs just because of the gassing problem. Only thing with the C-4, it was hard to light. But we found that if you pinch a little "tit" onto a piece of that white plastic C-4, it was easier to light there. It burns really, really hot though. We burnt a hole in a coffeepot one time, but we learned that if you took the ball of the C-4 and rolled it around in the dirt real good, it would burn slower. I was also told that if you stomped on it while it was burning, it'd blow up. Ha! I wonder who figured that out!

Back to Trioxane Trixie. In October, she began disappearing for a day or so at a time. Nobody knew where she'd gone to. We were feeding her enough, because she was as fat as a butterball, although a couple times we caught her partaking from one of the four holer's cans after it'd been burnt. Then one day while we were all in the Ops bunker playing cards, Trixie showed up, bumping into everything. Walking into chairs or boxes or whatever, the dog was hilariously funny to look at and watch, but it was absolutely pitiful at the same time. The dog's head was swelled up like a melon—featureless—little stubs for ears, a black place on the melon where the nose had been and eyes completely shut. It was amazing, but after several hours she completely cleared up.

Well, this happened several times and she continued to do her bumping into things, and flopping around trick. Then one day, our ARVN dancer (seems like it was Quan) was cooking a helmet of chow near the bunker's entrance. There was Trixie nosing up to the heat tab and sniffing it. It didn't take long and there was melon head banging, and flopping again. It seems our mountaintop pup had turned into a trioxane junkie.

ARVN SSgt Quan cooking some R&R—rat & rice. Courtesy of SgtMaj Joe Armstrong

DI DAH, DI DA DIT

11 The Triple "I"

JUST SITTING IN MY PIG PEN MANNING MY PIG (PRD-1) FOR hour after hour left a 20-year-old with a lot of time to think. I suppose I thought about everything a normal American boy thought about there in the first part of October of 1969, but especially did I think about my beautiful 20-year-old wife and baby daughter who were waiting for me back in South Florida. Linda had been my high school sweetheart since the tenth grade at Ft. Lauderdale High School. We had actually met in a church youth group which I really liked because there was a bunch of good looking girls in it. Our first date was the football homecoming game at the Orange Bowl Stadium in November 1964, between the Ft. Lauderdale High Flying 'L's and the Miami High

Honeymooning on Dad's boat in May 1968, Bahia Mar, Ft. Lauderdale, Fla.

Stingarees. It amazed me that I was so very fortunate to have such a girl love me and to have so excellent a baby daughter. God had sure smiled on me.

After Linda and I graduated from high school together, we drove out to the campus of Broward County Junior College to register in August 1967. However, I couldn't stand the thought of going to school anymore, at least for awhile, and had already talked to both the Navy and Marine recruiter. My father had been a sailor during WW II and told me a little about his time at Saipan, the Philippines and Okinawa. My background was from a very nautical family; Dad was the skipper on a 55-foot yacht, and I had grown up on the water, fishing, diving and skiing.

Having been a scuba diver since thirteen, it was my intention to go into a commercial diving career. I had even completed an introductory course, but the Navy recruiter didn't seem too positive about my chances to get into diving because I might not qualify. What, I might not qualify? Give me a break, sailor! I swam rings around every one of those guys who were regular students at that commercial diving school. If you talked to anybody in my high school graduating class of about 750 students, more than likely they would say, "Chuck Truitt, that's the guy you should talk to about anything to do with the ocean."

Recruiters, listen up! Because that Navy recruiter wasn't a little more positive, I tried the Marine recruiter who was standing there looking really sharp in that neat uniform at the entranceway of the office next door. He said something like, "Sure, we've got divers in the Marine Corps, and you look like you'd do great!" Wow, that's what this 18-year-old wanted to hear, so I took all of the tests and got everything ready just in case I couldn't force myself to sign up for another round of school. The day Linda and I went to register, I just couldn't do it. So, after dropping Linda off, I turned around, went straight

The eve of our first anniversary shortly after I informed Linda of my orders for Vietnam.

to the recruiter's office and signed on the dotted line. Besides, Vietnam was going full tilt and I was afraid that I'd miss out altogether if I didn't sign up soon.

I was stationed at Homestead, Florida, which was 61 miles from where I grew up. After about nine months on an accompanied tour with my new family, orders came in for 1st Radio Battalion. It was the 24th of May when my orders came in, and I had to leave in about three weeks to go to Staging at Camp Pendleton, California. That was also the date of Linda's and my first anniversary (notice all the joy and happiness in the picture). I was 19 years old and stupid, and therefore told Linda when I took her out for our anniversary dinner. She wore the new dress I had bought her with money earned from hunting snakes in the Everglades during my off time from Company "H" Marine stuff. SSgt Larry Robertson owned a pet shop in Perrine, and I used to hunt for all kinds of snakes and sell them to him. It wasn't much, but it sure augmented my meager income. Larry would give me a buck a foot for rattlesnakes over three feet or a buck apiece if they were less, $1.75 a foot for indigos, a buck apiece for water moccasins, about $3 a foot for king snakes and just plain old water snakes brought 25 cents each. Those water snakes are real nasty too; they were moccasin wanna-bees. The moccasins were just mean snakes, even meaner than I was, so I didn't usually fool with them as it just wasn't worth the hate and discontent.

Yeah, I thought about all that a lot up there on Dong Ha mountain. It sure had been a pain getting to where I was, and the only thing I could conclude was I was "A Child of the King" and "Jesus Loves Me," considering all He had done for me. Those all were my normal thoughts, but the situation at hand kept intruding into my mind.

FSB Fuller was having a rat body count taken every morning for the big contest to see who could get the five-day in-country R&R. Of course, rat traps were useless, or nonexistent, so we were devising other means of upping the body count, which for me meant the "Triple I," that is, imagination, innovation and initiative. We had a lot of goodies available to put the devices in use.

One of the goodies our bunch of 1st Radio Battalion warriors had was a machete. And one of the Triple I devices was a

FSB Fuller, looking South from the Northwest side, outside of the wire

Corporal Chuck Truitt sometime near the end of November or first part of December 1969.
—Courtesy of George Carnako

trap utilizing the machete to up our body count. A hole was designed into the handle for attaching a tether. As I sat there contemplating in the pig pen about how to rig that machete into an effective killing mechanism for rats, an idea was initiated. I took a big spike that was left over from making the bunkers and put it through the hole in the handle of the machete. That way it could be stuck into the wall and the blade would pivot on the spike. In all my cogitations, I thought about how to make an effective release mechanism. I used my big Buck knife to carve a notch into a small piece of wood which I tied to a cord and looped over one of the joints in the PSP runway matting from the roof of the bunker. With one end attached to the blade, then up to the PSP and back down to the wooden trip, I had the basic design thought out. A problem though was the fact that the machete blade wasn't heavy enough by itself to quickly and effectively dispatch a rat. No problem! We had lots of batteries. A couple of those BA-389, PRC-25 radio batteries and two BA-404s from the pig gave that blade plenty of weight. With the proper use of duct tape, and a little trial and error adjustments, the Triple I device was ready to be put in operation.

Our sleeping bunker was empty and undisturbed most of the time since everyone was away doing their SigInt thing. I set the trap and baited it with C-ration peanut butter, which I liberally smeared all over that piece of wood with the notch carved in it. Seemed like any self-respecting NVA rat just wouldn't be able to resist gnawing on the thing. That would release the cord from the notch and, in turn, allow the battery-weighted machete blade to fall and score its first KIA. It was all rigged right in front of a main rat hole near the floor at the entrance to the bunker.

It took a few tries, but I got that awkward rat cutter rigged. I left it and headed up to the pig pen, intending to return in a couple hours and give it a check. Well, I couldn't wait two hours. It was probably only 20 minutes before I made a quick run back down to check it out. I looked inside. Ha! It was sprung! Oh, rats! The only thing I got was a rattail and a blood trail. Well, I could work with the thing and tweak the mechanism to probably be more efficient. It might even be effective after awhile. However, I'd already imagined a completely different way!

Di Dah, Di Da Dit

12 Pop-Up Food Fight

(Betcha can't say that five times real fast!)

One hundred percent of our "BBs" (bullets, bandages and beans) came from the air via helicopter of some type or other. ("BBs" is the Marine's name for all supplies.) By the fall of 1969 the cloud cover was more and more; the common term for it was being "socked-in." In 1969, at the top of Dong Ha mountain we were socked-in a lot in late October, November and December too.

At no time did we ever run out of ammunition, but we certainly did run out of other stuff such as food and water. The highest and first priority for resupply was ammunition, bullets—the first "B" of "BBs." A lack of food was not really any big deal, but a lack of water was certainly the pits. On two different occasions we ran out of food—one time for two days and once for three days. Because I was such a big eater, it elicited a comment from Milford Cole, "If we run out of food one more time, I'm gonna shoot Truitt!" As a result (even though I believe it was in jest) I started eating most of my meals alone, taking my slop in my pig pen.

I believe Cole was just mad at me because of another incident. We played a lot of cards sitting in a circle in our Ops bunker in the dim light of a twisted wax candle from the 81mm mortar boxes. Usually there would be a couple guys, a linguist and a Morse operator "twisting the dials." Sometimes we would be playing hearts, or spades, but most often it was back alley. As we sat on the floor playing cards, those of us who chewed

Looking NNW from FSB Fuller towards Mutter's Ridge, Hill 484 and the DMZ.

tobacco would be spitting into a drink can. I had inadvertently set the half full can of spit down on the floor to my right between Cole and myself. In a little while Cole grabbed that can, thinking it was his drink. Well, you can imagine the commotion resulting from him taking a big swig of Redman spit.

There was a lot of food wasted, considering it all had to be transported up there, although I would say that the waste was much less than the average American's home. There's a lot of extra stuff in each C-ration box that we wouldn't use right away such as, accessory packs, little personal rolls of TP, cans of fruit, date nut and pecan nut rolls and some of the less desired main courses like canned ham and lima beans, and pork slices. I kinda liked them, if you fried them up real good first. Since we weren't always moving, we could store them. So what I'm saying is there were a lot of tidbits left over which we stored in our wooden ammo box seats.

There was never any problem eating food as long as we had it. If we wanted to eat just two, three or even four C's a day we

Cases of palletized C-rations on the beach at Chu Lai, ready for movement inland. Looks like Bob's got enough there to last him the rest of his tour. —Courtesy of Bob Page, a 1st RagBag Marine. In fact, that's him laying there in the shade.

could do it. But it was always just C-rations, which were augmented by what we got in the mail from home. Once a month, Linda went to the post office back home in Naranja to send a box of food. The mail clerk told her to just bring in the box unsealed. They would weigh, wrap and seal it right there at the max of 70 pounds. One time an army slick arrived and threw off several bags of mail for the whole FSB. One entire sealed mailbag was just for me. One of those boxes had broken open somewhere along the way and the post office had put it all in that individual bag. That was a really great care package.

There were also a couple KCS soldiers that had some chickens. I didn't even know they had them, and certainly didn't know how they kept the chickens quiet and hidden. Quan had acquired some eggs from them which he mixed in with something or other, possibly his special R&R meal (rat and rice); it was kind of like egg drop soup and it tasted great.

When the army took over from the 4th Marines and our 1st Radio Battalion guys were still up there, we often had the benefit of eating one of their daily (weather permitting) hot meals that came in from a chow hall somewhere around Quang Tri. Those army people would allow us Marines to stand in the chow line with all those soldiers. It would be regular chow hall food brought up in 155mm or 175mm ammo tubes, and it was usually still warm. Though it would be dished up right next to our bunker, the line would start way down in the artillery section and snake on up across the LZ. At least we didn't have far to go once we got it. Their first sergeant would be yelling something like, "*If you wanna eat, stand in line and stay five meters apart and zip up them flack jackets! Awright, spread it out, spread it out. You there—yeah, you with your flack jacket unzipped—get out of line and go to the rear!*"

Food was always dreamed about and a topic of conversation; seems like there was always someone talking about their mom's or their wife's cooking, or some restaurant or other. We even made plans to start our own restaurants. There was one plan to start a restaurant named the Bunker, made from sandbags filled with concrete. The menu would consist of C-rations, and it would be just candlelights. We'd have recordings of periodic "incomings" including loud booms that would shake the place and cause the candle flames to jump off the wick, just like the real thing. I wonder if anyone ever made a restaurant like that? I suppose it would have to be in a very big city, with a lot of advertising to get new customers all the time. For sure, there wouldn't be many return customers.

Gotta tell you a story here now. Sometimes the things we did for amusement involved food (even Marines at war have to have fun, and we definitely did, sometimes). Our signal and flare devices, commonly called "pop-ups," were each compacted into an aluminum tube that had a charge to shoot the integral rocket motor and pyrotechnic up into the air. If my memory serves me correctly, each tube was about an inch to one-and-a-third inches in diameter and about ten inches long. One end had an aluminum cap with a little firing pin, like a small nail or tack sticking up in the bottom. The way it worked

Pop flares—we called them "pop-ups." I love these things!

was to pull the cap off, revealing a painted cork plug (the color of the pyro), and then put that cap over the other end where there was a primer at the base of the tube. By pointing the tube up and away, then striking the cap, the propelling charge would blow the whole thing upward—the rocket motor, integral folding fins, pyrotechnic and all—then the little rocket would further propel it several hundred feet further into the air.

I used to take everything apart to see how it worked. Needless to say, a lot of things were field stripped: claymores, hand grenades and pop-ups, as well as many other things. The claymores had C4 plastic explosive inside, and the hand grenades had a yellow hard pressed powder called Composition B. Sometimes I could even get the things back together in working order. (Any of you guys remember field stripping M-26 fragmentation grenades to make 'yard bracelets from the serrated bands? "Oh no Gunny. We wouldn't do that!" Yeah, right! I sure saw a lot of guys wearing frag-band type 'yard bracelets.) It just

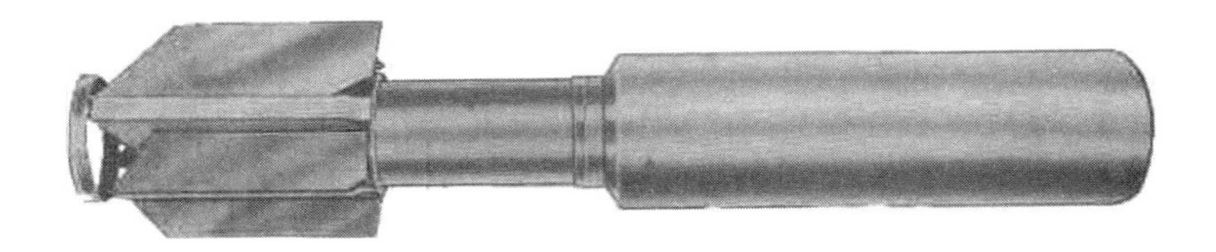

A pop-up rocket motor, w / pyrotechnic.

so happens that if you pop the cork and remove the rocket motor and pyrotechnic from a pop-up, it makes a great food launcher. If you pack a bunch of ham and limas, or pork slices with ketchup and tomato sauce into the tube, it can be shot out with a splat. Needless to say, upon occasion, someone or another would get blasted upside the head with a pork slice or something. Man, I really hated those hard lima beans!

In September and October before the 3rd MarDiv left Vietnam, I'd often watch the air show which was quite interesting at times. One of the really effective tactics used by my Marine brothers was when they'd "troll for gooks." A huey loaded with "sniffer gear" would fly low over the jungle using on-board equipment to detect enemy activity. More often than not, the detection was as a result of their receiving ground fire. They'd hear the gooks shooting at them, especially if any of the rounds started plinking into the bird.

It was pretty neat to watch them from our mountaintop perch. They'd be trolling out below us there, up and down, back and forth in the valleys, trying to get some of the "little people" to bite. The whole deal was that after they would sniff out the bad guys, two high-flying Cobra gunships would zoom in and "waste the area" with on-board ordinance, which was considerable. Those Cobras carried 2.75 inch rockets attached in pods on the

That's the gunpod under the nose of a Cobra gunship. See the 40mm automatic grenade launcher and the minigun with the red cowl, which is being worked on. That minigun will shoot either 3000 or 6000 rounds of 7.62mm rounds a minute. It sounds like a chainsaw. I was impressed!

The 2.75 inch rockets that were mounted on both sides of a Cobra gunship.

sides of the aircraft. They also had a multi-barreled Gatling-type gun, which we knew as a minigun, and it could fire either 3,000 or 6,000 rounds a minute. This is much faster than a regular M-60 M/G which fired about 600 to 700 rounds a minute. There was also a 40mm grenade launcher that spewed out a lot of fire-power as well. Both the minigun and grenade launcher were mounted on a gun pod, hung under the nose of the Cobra. It was all aimed by the gunner who simply had to look at the target and shoot, because the aiming mechanism was coordinated with the eyepiece in the gunner's helmet. I suppose it was always good not to be holding down the trigger while sneezing. Ha!

Several months later, we were visiting with my folks on my dad's boat, The Pagan Too, while on leave after Vietnam. It was a still, misty morning at the end of August 1970, and they were docked at a Yacht Club in Shadyside, Maryland, for the summer. I distinctly remember sitting in serenity, looking out towards the dark tree line across the West River. In my mind's eye, I can still see those little spirals of steam rising, as an ominous noise wafted across the still, mirrored surface of the water. I said, "Dad, that noise sounds just like a Cobra 'working out' his minigun." It was a man cutting a tree with a chainsaw. There was no difference; they sounded exactly the same.

Those air shows came to an abrupt halt when the Army replaced the Marines. Their FAC requirements were handled by the USAF called "Barky." It seems that, for a period of time at least, "Barky" birds weren't allowed to fly lower than 1500 feet (the correct term of which escapes me, AGL or something like that) and I presume their other air operations were under the same restriction. Regardless, when the Marines left, a lot of the interesting air shows were eliminated, as well as that effective tactic the Marines had been using. Is it any wonder that after the Marines left, more and more control of the northern "I" Corps area was lost to the NVA? Oh, I'm sure some folks will argue with that, but the facts remain clear. As long as the Corps was there and Corps tactics were used, the NVA was held at bay.

For sure, our pop-up food fights went a long way towards subduing an aggressive enemy!

Di Dah, Di Da Dit

13 Radio, Panasonic, Boiled, 1-Each

I WAS SITTING IN MY PIG PEN ON TOP OF OUR BUNKER ON FSB Fuller around the end of October 1969. It was pretty cool up there on top of that mountain. The pig pen was about five feet by six feet and about four feet high, and made of sandbags all the way around. At one end sat the PRD-1 (we called it the "pig") on a tripod stand with just the "merry-go-round" and directional antenna sticking up above the sandbags. It was necessary to

Cpl Chuck Truitt and ARVN Dancer SSgt Quan

climb in from the top and over the sandbags. That is where I'd sit for hours on a stool using the pig to get DF shots on radio signals whenever Net Control in Dong Ha would call in a mission. Sometimes we were really busy for long periods at a time, other times it was terribly slow. The other 1st Radio Battalion guys and dancers worked in the operations bunker underneath me. I spent a lot of time standing up between the pig and the four-foot sandbagged wall, just gazing out with an unobstructed view in all directions, daydreaming and just thinking. It was absolutely gorgeous; and that's a 20-year-old talking too, remember? I wasn't even old enough to really appreciate flowers and beautiful things yet. You know how it was at 20 years old, "*Yeah, yeah that's real pretty*"—stuff like that, but I do remember it was beautiful on Dong Ha mountain. That is, when we weren't socked in by the clouds at that altitude of 549 meters.

Thermite Incendiary Grenade

The half of the pig pen that I sat under was covered with engineer's stakes, plastic sheeting, and sandbags. Stuck in behind me were lots of pig batteries (seems like BA 404s and 419s, plus batteries for my PRC-25 R/T—BA 386s) also one thermite grenade, my deuce gear (combat gear), bandoleers of ammo, a clacker, and a coil of wire. I believe it was up on FSB Russell that they were overrun by the NVA, and the guys had to destroy their pig. They set off three thermite incendiary grenades, but those things just burnt holes down through the pig. Therefore, I had my pig wired here on Fuller. I had a claymore mine taped to the back of the thing with duct tape. My plan was that if we were overrun, I'd set off the thermite on top of the pig, then fall back to a pre-planned position. If some of the "little people" got near the pig, then I'd squeeze the clacker, hoping that it would work better than it had earlier with the rats. Regardless, between the

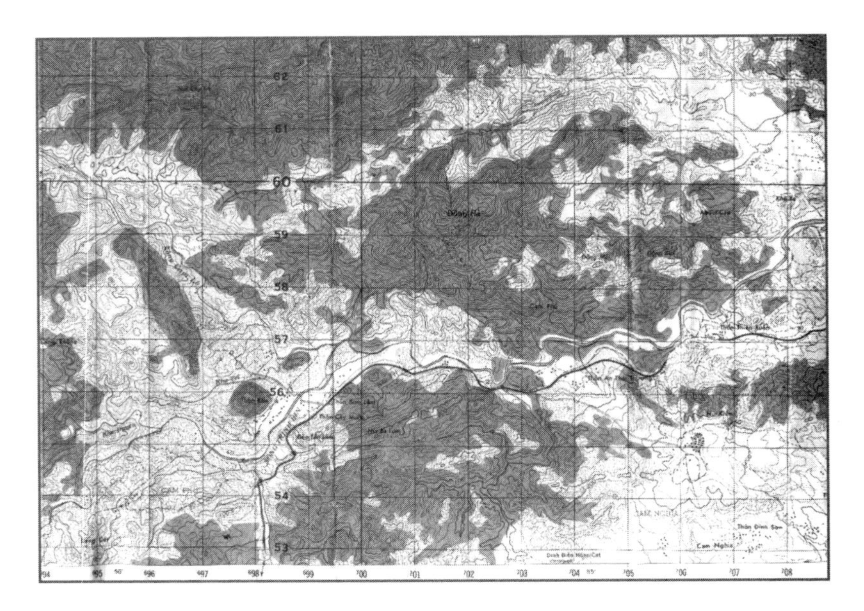

thermite and the claymore, that pig would end up as well-done pieces of bacon.

As I sat under the low overhead, by leaning forward from my stool, the dial and controls of the pig could be operated. Then by spinning the "merry-go-round" on top with the antenna on it and throwing down the back-azimuth lever as well, I could get an azimuth—shot—on the radio transmission. While whiling away the hours, I often listened to AFVN on my little portable Panasonic transistor radio, or Hanoi Hannah (you know the bit—"*Sorry U. S. Marines, but today the Song Ben Hai ran red with blood from your brothers of the 3rd Marine Division*"—or some other completely bogus, ridiculous announcement meant to influence impressionable, little, deluded girls like Jane Fonda). The radio was hung right in front of my head by its leather tether from the overhead engineer stakes.

Well, one day I was heating up a helmet full of water for some C-ration hot chocolate, using a small chunk of C4. It was all sitting right in front of me between my feet, with the pig just a short arm's reach ahead. The water had gotten very hot, maybe boiling, and I had just ripped open the package to dump the powder into the pot, when all of a sudden on the PRC-25 speaker, from Net Control in Dong Ha, I heard *"All Stations, All Stations, this is Florida Vacation Alpha, with a message on Mike, Mike..."* which meant that it was time to put my pig to work. Quickly, I grabbed my Comus pad (a one-time encryption pad) and marked the correct doodahs, to find the exact frequency and all the pertinent info. In a flash, I leaned forward to spin the dials and the "merry-go-round."

Smack, my head hit the little Panasonic radio which fell straight into my helmet of boiling water. Well, my priority was

Looking south from my pig pen; notice the trash chute and the salient towards the West.

getting the shot on the enemy target ASAP, which may only have been viable for just a few seconds. After sending my traffic back to Dong Ha, I retrieved the radio from the pot between my feet. It was my hope that since it was just hot water, possibly that transistor radio would still work after a change of batteries and thorough drying out. No such luck! So, it got the heave-ho down the big conduit trash chute that launched it several hundred feet down the west side of the mountain.

Apropos was that little ditty we used to sing,

We like it here, we like it here,
You bet your butt we like it here!
And though we're down with malaria,
We still police the area!

And, there's a hundred more verses too.

How about this song?

Going home in a body bag
Doo dah, doo dah,
Going home in a body bag,
Oh da doo dah de.

You know what? "It Don't Mean Nuthin!"

Di Dah, Di Da Dit

14 The Exotic Harvest Moon

THE MARINE CORPS BIRTHDAY OF 10 NOVEMBER 1969 WILL forever be an indelible memory in my "brain housing group." I have participated in some really memorable Marine Corps birthdays. For instance, I'll never forget my first Marine Corps birthday on 10 November 1967; it was the time of the harvest moon. That particular Marine Corps birthday was when two drunken drill instructors came through our recruit barracks and proceeded to "thump" myself and the other fire watch at "0 dark

The 1972 Color Guard in Scotland w/Sgt Truitt as the NCOIC (carrying the American flag).

30" hours because we didn't sound the alarm as the two of them snuck up on us. Since I had let my whole platoon down by supposedly getting them all killed, I lost my position as a squad leader, and possibly platoon honor man. A week later, at boot camp graduation, my wife could verify all my bruises, especially the ones under each of the large utility jacket buttons on my chest. But, that's okay since they were hardening us up for combat in Vietnam where most of us recruits would be going shortly after infantry training. I guess I just didn't realize that I was supposed to wake up the whole platoon and warn them of two drunken DIs.

Some other memorable Marine Corps birthdays were in Scotland, when we had the Royal Marine band playing for us in 1970, '71, and '72. It was also a great Marine Corps Birthday Ball at Company "K," Pensacola in 1975 when I was a SSgt instructor there. I had been there the year before as well, but that year I had Jon Wuerffell and his wife Lola as our guests. The Marine ceremony had all the different period uniforms, and

The Royal Marine Band in Scotland playing for the U.S. Marine Corps Birthday Ball on 10 November 1971.

our C.O.'s sword was stuck in its scabbard. Seems that it hadn't been drawn since the Birthday Ball of the previous year, and the PFC who had put it back in the scabbard then hadn't wiped the cake's icing off first.

Jon Wuerffell was a scuba diving partner of mine, and he was also an assistant pastor of a church in Pensacola. I'd started night diving with him in the fall when the Escambia Bay water started to cool down, and the flounder began running out of Pensacola Pass into the deeper and warmer Gulf waters. Our night dives were usually after 2300 when I got off duty, and each of us would usually get a nice stringer of flounder in the three- to seven-pound or sometimes even larger class. You see, those flounder didn't know what color to turn, or how to properly camouflage themselves at night, and a good diver with a dive light could usually come in with a right fair take. There was a catch though, as "there is no free lunch." The upper Gulf of Mexico is one of the "sharkiest" places I've ever dove in, and I've dove a lot all over the world. The first time I ever ate bull shark was after a night dive there near the Fort Pickins pier where a guy caught a huge monster shark right where we were harvesting flounder on a nearly full moon night.

It wasn't long after attending our Marine Corps Birthday Ball that Jon Wuerffell joined the Air Force; it musta been the "stuck sword trick" that pushed him in that wayward direction towards the "dark side." Yeah, seems like it was about that time that the movie "Star Wars" came out too. By the way, his son Danny—a little rug-rat then—would be the University of Florida's quarterback sensation twenty or so years later, and then a quarterback for the Washington Redskins.

Back to Vietnam: I was given three sets of camouflage "jungle utilities" (cammies) when initially arriving in DaNang. They were certainly different than our normal sateen utilities. Much baggier and with more freedom of movement, they were very comfortable. They had slanted pockets on the breast which made it easier to access when wearing other gear such as a flack jacket, and those big carrying pockets on the legs were great too.

All cammies had one major deficiency though, as I believe the procurement for materials to make them was truly a lowest-bidder-type deal. The problem wasn't in the overall design of the cammies, but in the poor quality of the zipper. The old button fly on our regular utilities was far superior to those zippers on the cammies. By the end of the first week or two at VCB all three sets of cammies had broken zippers, and it wasn't just mine either. I am confident that every Marine in Vietnam with cammies had a broken zipper, therefore every Marine's zipper was open. Think about that just a moment: 100 percent of the Marine Corps in Vietnam went around all the time with broken zippers, and 90 percent of them (except the rear echelon-type people) wore no skivvies. Maybe that's where they got the expression, "let it all hang out!"

At Vandergrift we somehow had our cammies cleaned upon occasion (seems like maybe the "yards" washed them in the stream), but no one ever wore skivvies. Personally, I had about three sets of white skivvies, and when they all got dirty I put them all in a C-ration box, along with some other stuff, and mailed them back home. Neither making mention of them, nor telling Linda to just wash and put them away, I received my cleaned and folded skivvies again in a care package with some other goodies from her a few weeks later. Ha! She later told me, "Honey, I was just being a dutiful and compliant wife."

By mid-September 1969, FSB Fuller was my humble abode for awhile. The only water up there was brought in via helicopter; any type of laundering of clothing was not even thought of. Basic hygiene was mostly just the brushing of teeth—for weeks at a time—until making a resupply run to Dong Ha, or when leaving for some other reason. At 1800 feet altitude the temperature was never hot, and as it got later in the year there was more and more cloud cover.

An NVA flag and an AK-47 captured from one of the caves on Dong Ha mountain. —Courtesy of E. F. Quigley

There was never a good and proper rain while I was there; most always it was a very fine mist that would come whipping sideways across the top of that mountain. I remember that I got so filthy after several weeks that I would rub areas on my arms and wrists, to get the dirt up into little balls and then flick them off. Once, around the first or second week in October, it started to rain, the real thing too, so I took the opportunity to strip off all my clothes and soap down. Just about that time the rain abruptly stopped—NOT NICE—I was very uncomfortable for awhile. By the time I left FSB Fuller around February 1970 I'd had two-and-a-half showers. Twice was on runs back to Dong Ha, and the half was my truncated shower in the rain.

In October I had developed some type of fungal growth on both knees and the back of my left leg about four inches above and behind my knee. Now I'm not talking about your basic skin irritant or fungus. I'm talking about some real nasty stuff that caused deep oozing, open sores, almost like abscesses. The corpsman said it was "jungle rot" and he gave me some Phisohex liquid in a green plastic bottle, and a plastic brush with instruction to scrub it liberally a couple times a day. That was absolutely miserable as I'd scrub, and the blood would just run down my legs, then I'd rinse it with water from my canteen cup. It would not go away, and stayed with me for several months. I finally made mention of it in a letter home, and a few weeks later a small bottle of medicine was received from my mom who had told a dermatologist in Ft. Lauderdale about it. After just a few days the wounds started to heal, but they were sure open and deep sores by then. (Thanks, Mom, I've always appreciated you for special stuff just like that.) Seems like I should have gotten a Purple Heart medal because for sure that was some kind of NVA

The Greek (next to the R/T) and a U/I soldier of the army's 407 RRD who would replace us in February '70. —Courtesy of "Fighting Joe" Armstrong.

fungus. About every twelve to eighteen months for several years after, there was a new eruption of the nasty stuff on the big hole that rotted away on the back of my leg. To this day, more than thirty-three years later, the scars are there and they get deep blue when my skin gets cold.

I had one set of cammies on when I arrived at Fuller, and I continued to wear them until they just wore out. I never took them off (except the time I got "half a shower"). In my little pig pen, while manning my "pig," a PRD-1 radio direction finder, I sat for hours on a rough wooden ammo box. As a result, the back side of those cammies got mighty thin and holes began appearing quickly; often even before the knees got holes. Remember they were filthy; they were so filthy, in fact, that they became pasty, and they would practically stand up by themselves.

So, as was the predicament of many of America's finest young men in similar situations in Vietnam, we were filthy, our trousers all had broken zippers, not one of us ever wore skivvies and many of us had holes in the seat of our pants. Well, after the first set became very unserviceable, I put on a new pair and gave the nasty ones the heave-ho down the trash chute. After a few weeks of 24/7 wear in that damp, filthy, rugged environment, the second set got the ol' heave-ho as well. I was down to my last fresh set of cammies, and by the 10th of November they were really nasty too.

With a broken zipper, no skivvies, filthy, nasty, stiff cammie trousers that had a hole in one knee and a large, substantial hole in the seat, I was beginning to get a little self-conscious, even up there with just men around and many in nearly the same predicament. Possibly it was the cool breeze in back always reminding me. Most of the guys who rotated on and off the mountain would be able to get serviceable cammies, but those of us who just stayed there, well, many of us had bare butts, to one degree or another.

It just so happens that our Brass wanted to spend the Marine Corps birthday with one of the battalion's forward units. I suppose we were about the most forward unit the battalion had. About mid-day on the 10th of November 1969 three of Rag Bag's officers "chopped" in on a Marine Huey, one of which was a major, the battalion's XO. Those guys were really great, because they brought us some goodies. I never imagined that there were canned hams in Vietnam, nor crackers and good cheese too (not that C-ration junk). Furthermore, they had a couple cases of beverages and two canteens of really special beverages. Needless to say, 1st Radio Battalion had an extra special Marine Corps birthday at Dong Ha mountain on the 10th of November 1969.

I tried to stay facing those officers or seated while they were there. In fact, one of my memories is the extra effort I made to keep them from seeing the "harvest moon." As it turned out, they ended up spending the night with us because they couldn't get another bird out; I'm sure that was half their plan anyhow. Ya know, them rear echelon-type people, who were usually stuck at DaNang, were looking for an excuse/opportunity to experience some of Vietnam's exotic camping opportunities. Well, they certainly got their exotic experience.

One totally filthy Chuck Truitt about mid-October 1969. The "harvest moon" was definitely shining from the right angle! Notice the defoliated trees!

The next day, all of us were feeling a little thick from the goodies they brought up; you

FSB Fuller above the clouds. —Courtesy of the 407th RRD

know, we just weren't accustomed to that rich ham, cheese and crackers and stuff. (*Stuff*, don't ya just love that word *stuff*, that's one of my favorite words; it explains a whole world of stuff.) Before they left, one of those Marines said to me, "I'll see what I can do about getting you some new trousers." I guess I could hide it for a little while, but due to the circumstances and the extended length of time, our situation was a little more than we could conceal from those guys for that long (I'm sure that you can read into this somewhat).

About a day later I got a real chewing out, via radio relay, from a SSgt in DaNang who was the battalion supply sergeant. He complained that I got him into trouble: "What a maggot!" I suppose that I'd have punched him in the nose if he'd been close enough. Several days later I received two sets of trousers, size extra large and plain green like the army had. Fine! Now I had a grotty cammie jacket, and plain green, very baggie, doggie style trousers (man, I'd a punched that guy). Then I had to use a claymore bag strap to keep the trousers tied up around my waist. Well, at least the cool draft was gone and I no longer had to be self-conscious about inadvertently increasing anyone's exotic experience.

DI DAH, DI DA DIT

15 When Grown Men Cry

My job in Vietnam was SigInt which was a very effective and important job. It required a lot of formal military schooling, and a top secret security clearance as well. Whenever guys changed duty stations or were transferred from one unit to another, that security clearance had to be transferred with them. Sometimes, due to any number of reasons, it took several months and that could hold up the clearance. In the meantime,

Somewhere, out there, to the NE of FSB Fuller is A4, the DMZ, and the bad guys.

when a person was transferred and his clearance hadn't arrived yet, he was put to work doing some other type of job. Sometimes he would be assigned to just mundane chores or assigned to the Motor-T section, or some other type of job that needed to be done, but not necessarily by a someone that had a TS clearance. For some reason, in my whole 14 years in the Marine Corps, I was never held up as my clearance was always close on my heels. A security clearance is a very valuable thing; it needs to be protected. A person who has one needs to keep himself in such a manner that will not put his clearance status in jeopardy; similar to how we should protect our wives, children and loved ones from being in compromising situations or danger. "Sometimes

CH-47, Chinook with an external load of BBs.

ya just gotta say No! ya know, just for protection." In Vietnam I was put to work right away in my SigInt job. There are a lot of different aspects to SigInt, but I felt so very fortunate to work HFDF which was what I wanted to do more than anything else in the world at that time.

A Marine CH-53 w/external 105mm howitzer.

Once, after locating a nearby enemy unit with our DF, an artillery fire mission was called. After the "splash," a patrol of some strength was sent out to investigate. We ended up with a captured ChiCom radio. It was that "puke green" Chinese army color (every piece of Chinese gear I ever saw was that same yucky color), and the radio had two M-16 holes right near the top. Interestingly, both rounds passed through the radio without hitting anything of importance inside before they took the operator's head off. The radio still worked perfectly. It was voice capable, and had a BFO which made it useful for Morse code operations as well. Not only that, it had an integral Morse key built in, right on the side. What a neat piece of gear! The gook was wearing it strapped on his back when he died, and there was blood all over the thing and the headset had blood and chunks, but it still worked, and we used it.

In late November 1969 the switch had already been made. First Radio Battalion had the only Marines left on the mountain. The 4th Marines (4th Marine Regiment) were gone completely from Vietnam, and doggies from the 1st Brigade of the 5th Mechanized Division had replaced them. Now, Dong Ha mountain sat right in the middle of "Injun Country." On the east side was Leatherneck Square, to the north was Mutter's Ridge, the "Z" and then North Vietnam. To our south was an area of dense jungle, then the Khe Gio bridge, and highway 9 which ran from Dong Ha to the rockpile. On the west was the Razorback, then mountains and on in to Laos. It was a wild and wooly country where we were at, with free fire zone in every direction.

Because of the cloud cover, sometimes we could hear the birds overhead as they orbited and looked for a hole in the clouds to come through. Sometimes we'd hear a resupply bird overhead for awhile just trying to get in, and then they'd shoot down to the LZ, through just a slight hole. There was never any difficulty taking off again as there was nothing else to run into.

During late October, when a hole in the clouds appeared over Fuller, a bird landed. Come to find out, a chaplain had chopped in from some rear area and decided to hold religious services. Being a very baby Christian, even though saved at 13 years old, I did not realize that real born-again Christian chaplains, who really knew

An Army CH-47 Chinook (hook) with BBs.

the Saviour, were the exception rather than the rule. There is a very real difference in being very religious, as compared to having trusted in Jesus Christ for salvation, you know. In any case, that religious man announced that he was going to hold services. I thought, that's great! I want to do that. So, close to the LZ, the chaplain gathered around all who wanted to participate. We were sitting on the edge of bunkers, the ground or wherever we found convenient while he stood and started off with the service. I was flabbergasted when that guy began by telling a dirty joke! I couldn't believe it. Supposedly it was to get everyone's attention, but I want you to understand that he didn't need to get anyone's attention; he already had our undivided attention. I'll never forget that. How dare that chaplain profane such an important occasion as a worship service of Jesus Christ. Needless to say, I attended no more services ever while I was in Vietnam; not that there was a plethora of chaplains who ever made it to the boondocks anyhow. The ones that did make it out were usually sightseers. (Note: For 17 years now, I have pastored a church on Okinawa whose members include people from all branches of the military. During this time I have met and dealt with some excellent chaplains, and even had a couple in to preach. Unfortunately, the chaplain's corps still has more than its share of guys like that one in Vietnam.)

Our "BBs" were not near as consistent in November. We had so far run out of food two different times before being resupplied. But that was nothing. It was when we ran out of water that wasn't nice. Three times we ran out. The first time was just for a day, then the second time was for two days. Yeah, you guessed it, the third time was for three days, and that was really the pits too.

There was a guy there that had a big appetite—it was me—I was a big eater, and rarely were there any additions from me to the wooden ammo boxes which we used to store uneaten C-rations. In fact, it was more likely to be me withdrawing from the hoard,

This is one type of PSP (perforated steel plate); some other types had smaller holes

rather than adding to it. I was always glad to get it, and being a Christian, I always thanked the Lord for it. But you know, I don't ever remember thanking Him for my drink. At least not until November 1969. In fact, nearly everyone that knows me today knows that I always thank Him for both my food and drink.

On this particular occasion our resupply of water became very interesting as the story unfolded. We could hear the resupply birds orbiting but they couldn't break through the cloud barrier. The first bird, a CH-47 (an army Chinook), made it down in the late morning or early afternoon, and he had a water bull slung from beneath. Engineer stakes were sticking up all the way around the LZ with rope strung from one to the next, so that no one would get blown over the side from a chopper's considerable wash; those choppers really "break wind," ya know!

Being the third day without any water, everyone was excited and watching as the water bull set down on the LZ. One of the men unharnessed the tether, amidst cheers, while the bird hovered above. As the harness was released, the bird sunk down just a little more before departing, and the hook and tether slipped down along the side of the bull. Then as the bird took off, up and away, the tether somehow snagged the side near the wheel, and the whole water bull completely flipped over right there on the LZ. Luckily, the guy who released the tether had jumped clear, escaping injury as the bird departed. As you can probably imagine, the water rapidly evacuated out of the large hatch (big enough for a grown man to easily enter for inspection and maintenance) in the inverted top, flowed down through the PSP and slurried down along the sides of the mountain.

There was sure a bunch of disappointed guys watching with interest; the cheers had turned to moanings and groanings, and cursings. Several of them right there tried to catch the nasty stuff in hastily acquired containers before it was completely gone; those had to be some really thirsty, dry throats to consider partaking of that nasty stuff. I have to hand it to that pilot, he was very sympathetic, and though I wasn't privy to the actual radio conversation, he made us aware that he would not quit, but that he would be sure we got a load of water. Probably within an hour, we could hear that same bird, or another Chinook orbiting overhead looking for a hole to drop through. I can't remember any other birds making it in during the interval.

Suddenly the bird appeared, though we could hear it for awhile. There was no water bull, but this time it was a water blivet. That big, black balloon full of water was swinging a bit as it was about to settle onto the LZ. Wouldn't you just know it?

Notice the rubber water blivet (water container) on the other side of the LZ; this picture was taken at least a month before the Army arrived on Fuller in November of 1969 and installed engineer stakes around the LZ.

That blivet struck an engineer stake and split wide open. Once again the precious liquid dispersed down through the PSP and all down everywhere, and in much greater torrents even than the last time. That's when I saw grown men cry! To me it seemed those soldiers hadn't even been in-country long enough to get thirsty.

How long would this cloud cover last? For the third appearance the wait was a bit longer. Possibly the pilot was having difficulty locating a suitable container that was ready to go. Finally the bird showed up once more, and made it through with no delay or problems. Again it was a blivet, and it was set down on the LZ. Then the bird departed, and everything was copasetic just as if there had never been any problems at all.

Ever since November 1969, I have always thanked the Lord for both my food and my drink before I eat, and often whenever I have a drink between meals do I offer up a silent prayer as well. I mean, even a dog will thank his master with a lick or a wag. Should we do any less? I guess sometimes we just need to have had been in a position to appreciate things.

DI DAH, DI DA DIT

16 An Eerie Sucking Sound

By mid-November 1969, atop Dong Ha mountain there in the Republic of Vietnam, things had changed greatly from just a few weeks earlier. As time moved on, the weather became cooler, and there was beau coup (a lot) more cloud cover. I had mixed emotions about the whole situation. I loved being there and especially working DF. Yet, on an immediate and local level, it seemed that the wind quit making the usual woooing sounds. Rather, it seemed to make an eerie sucking sound as it blew down across Mutter's Ridge and the DMZ from the communist north or from Leatherneck Square to the east. All of a sudden we were the only Marines there on the mountain. The army had arrived in the next step of our president's plan of Vietnamization. My mixed emotions, or ambivalence, was that I loved my job, but at the same time the situation was the pits. It was kinda like playing sports such as football and motocross. I loved the sports, both in high school and later years. I played hard too, but you gotta pay the price. For instance, I've managed to have sixteen broken bones in thirteen separate incidents. I loved the activities, but sometimes they hurt. And that's how it was in Vietnam.

It really was an important job. After all, we were fighting to keep the aggressor communists of the north from taking over the country. Looking back upon it now from a different perspective or point of view, I can also see that America's expenditure of blood and bucks ended up helping to stop the advance of communism

Chuck Truitt about mid-September—not too skinny yet, not too much hair—probably not too filthy and smelly.

on a worldwide level. We drained them and even the giant Soviet Union was defunct in twenty years.

During the day of November 17, our own 1st Radio Battalion's SigInt efforts produced an incident very reminiscent of the one that greatly influenced the American victory at the Battle of Midway in WW II. In this particular event we found that a NVA regiment (my memory seems to tell me it was the 246th of the 304th Division) was in comms with an NVA arty unit—a combination that always spelled t-r-o-u-b-l-e for someone. Whenever any part of the 304th was on the move, somebody was going to die. And, amazingly it was "them" that always got hit way harder than us, but they'd just *didi mau* back across the DMZ or into Laos. There they just regrouped, resupplied, rebuilt and retrained with immunity their devastated elements, while awaiting another time to create hate and discontent. We could never receive permission to follow in hot pursuit.

So the big question was, who would that lucky somebody be? Well, we had a tri-nome indicator that signaled who that somebody was that would have the honors. It's just that we weren't exactly sure who the three number indicator indicated.

Possibly the tri-nome was C2, a fire support base that was just a little to our east, or possibly the Khe Gio bridge near the southern base of our mountain. It could also be Camp Elliot at the rockpile, but then again, it could just as well be us. Not knowing who, caused us all to spin the dials on our radios more intently and I was purposed to locate them with my pig (PRD-1 direction finder) atop our bunker in the pig pen.

Every American unit in the whole northern "I" Corps area was alerted that something was up. Everyone was on standby to assist the "chosen somebodies." Every arty unit that could push out a round far enough with maximum charge was ready to participate. Every air unit was standing by to render assistance, even though the cloud cover was heavy and no aircraft could drop bombs without possibly hitting the good guys.

Early in the evening, up in my pig pen, the speaker crackled, *"All Stations, All Stations this is Florida Vacation Alpha with a message on Bravo Zulu; stand by to receive traffic."* Net control at Dong Ha had a target for us. In just a short minute's time, I was

A 175mm gun of the type that supported us.

FSB C-2 —Courtesy of Rick Swan

sending my own traffic back which was a really good shot/bearing on the enemy transmission, whom I believe was the supporting artillery battalion. It seems that they were to provide artillery support for the 246th as that infantry regiment made its assault on the chosen somebody. But who was chosen? We'd all find out soon enough.

My memory gets a little fuzzy here, but I recall hearing the brouhaha from the big boys (155mm and 8 inch howitzers, and the 175mm guns) at Dong Ha, Alpha 4, Charlie 2 and Camp Carroll as they were firing on the enemy's arty, at least on their radio operator. Seems like everybody was getting in on the action. We thought we knew where their arty support was coming from, but we still had no location on the 246th, nor did we know who they were about to play "patty-cake" with. For some reason I recall going back down into our operations bunker—possibly because those big guns were impacting not too far from us (danger close) and the rounds, especially the 175s from

Camp Carroll were doing their freight train impressions as they passed just over our heads. Just a slight miscalc or a short round would create beau coup "hate and discontent" right in our own perimeter. Some days I'd hear our 1st RagBag DF guy at Camp Carroll talking on our net radio frequency when the 175s right near him would start shooting in our direction. Then he'd say something like, "Hey, Foxtrot [that's us at Fuller], you've got some big boys heading your way," and sure enough, those 175 rounds would go roaring by. On this occasion, I recall being told across the radio that they were firing some kind of pattern to saturate the suspected target area with steel. Not being an artilleryman, was the term "shooting iron crosses" or something like that?

Regardless, for whatever reason, we were all in the bunker as Camp Carroll's 175s were doing their fly-by. Those of us who were not actually on the radio (seems like our dancers were the ones spinning the dials) were playing back alley. I distinctly remember that at 2130 hours we were all actively discussing who was going to get hit. All of a sudden I remembered that all my deuce gear was in our sleeping bunker next door. That required my leaving the entrance to our bunker, traversing the ledge and going into the other bunker to retrieve my flack jacket and junk. I recall standing at the entrance and saying, "Who's it gonna be."

An 8" howitzer at Con Thien —Courtesy of Rick Swan

"Not us," came the consensus, though the dancers weren't saying much, but seemed rather shook up. One step along towards the other bunker, just one step and all of a sudden a great big KA-WAAAM. An RPG impacted right on the other side of the bunker entrance where I was headed. I felt the concussion, but continued into the other bunker after just a slight pause, during which time I yelled back into the Ops bunker, "It's us!"—as if they hadn't already figured that out. Those RPGs were not accurate at all past fifty to a hundred yards, but they could be used as an indirect fire weapon for distances out to nine hundred yards or so. After the retrieval of my combat gear, to include my M-79, I went back to the operations bunker where my rifle and all the other guys were. Then NVA 82mm mortars started dropping in on us, but kind of spread out, not nearly as heavy as I expected.

My memory is sketchy here, because I remember at some time being along our sandbagged wall awaiting an enemy assault, as well as being in the operations bunker. I also remember that

Near the NW perimeter wall with some cloud cover, although that clearing is about 350 yards west on top of the ridge.

we could hear the wonderful sound of the flares as they'd pop overhead, but we just couldn't tell exactly where they were because of the thick cloud cover. We were definitely socked-in. In the bunker with our radios we could tune in to any frequency, one of which I recall was the "basketball ship"—a large aircraft that kept orbiting overhead and dropping large drum-sized flares. He stayed there for hours always keeping a flare in the air, and when one would leave, another would take his place. Sometimes when a flare would be dropped a little too far away or it'd drift too far, one of our 81mm mortars would pop a flare and there would be more light. It was always really eerie though as the parachutes would float down through the clouds. Sometimes they'd be real close and we'd hear the sizzle, feel the heat and smell the fumes as they'd float by, then sputter and extinguish, sometimes just right there. I remember getting the call to return to my pig pen to get some RDF shots. The pig was the very highest point on the mountain, and I could see a full 360 degrees all around—for a few feet that is, because of the clouds. That's really eerie you know, people trying to kill you and your not being able to see anything.

Just a little after the NVA mortars started coming in on us we got the word from Dong Ha that the enemy 246th regiment would no longer be supported in their assault by the assigned artillery unit. Seems that they had been decimated by American artillery. Ha! That means that we had saved our own butts! Our own radio direction finding had located and caused our own big guns and howitzers to deliver steel on the enemy so that they

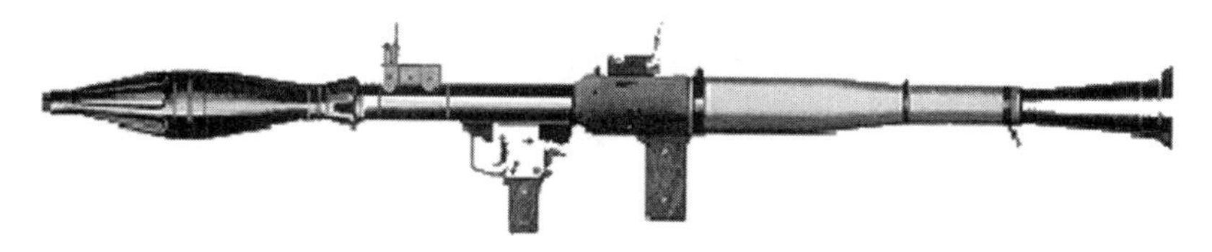

An RPG-7 (B-41) with rocket grenade sticking out of the end.

could not support the ground assault. Evidently the 82s that were falling on us were indigenous to the NVA 246th regiment, because the artillery unit we had destroyed probably would have used rockets and howitzers.

The mortars fell throughout the night, and an occasional RPG came slamming into something. However, the expected ground assault never materialized into anything that caused major concern, because as soon as we realized that we were the lucky somebodies, every arty unit within range started pumping steel in patterns all around our perimeter. The crescendo was intense at first, but abated after awhile. I was told the next day that more than a hundred dud 82mm NVA mortar rounds with their fins sticking up had been dropped into our perimeter by the enemy. Possibly they were defective, maybe they just weren't detonating in the fine, misty rain and moisture-softened earth. I know there were a lot that weren't duds too.

The next morning, the 18th of November 1969 as the light stabbed through the heavy clouds, all enemy activity had been completely non-existent for a few hours. There were no KIAs of ours and the WIAs were staged by the LZ to be medevaced as soon as a bird could get in. We could hear them overhead, above the cloud cover, watching for a hole. There were several of them, just orbiting around.

A Bell TH-13, this is what brought the Donut Dollies.

Red Cross Donut Dollies. —Courtesy 407 RRD

Ah, a hole appeared and zoom, in no time at all a bird shot in and set right down on that little LZ. It was unlike any bird that I had seen yet in Vietnam. There were still several birds up above us but out of sight as it was a very fleeting hole. The pilot disembarked as well as the one, possibly two, passengers. Ha! I couldn't believe my eyes. It was a civilian pilot, and a Donut Dollie in her pretty blue dress. Possibly there were two of them, although, as I think back upon it, it doesn't seem like that whirlybird was big enough to carry a pilot and two people. Regardless, they were there for a very short time before an army officer ran up screaming, "Get out of here. Get out of here!" We had WIAs staged by the LZ awaiting a medevac to find a hole in the clouds. One of the WIAs was a lieutenant with a piece of steel shrapnel in his forehead. We needed BBs and stuff as well. Finally a hole broke and what did we get? A sightseeing Donut Dollie! My memory mainly sees the blue dress and the soldier running up with his arms waving. If she'd stuck around, maybe she would have seen the "harvest moon."

DI DAH, DI DA DIT

17 The Vinh Dai Jeep Crusher

This story really starts in the storeroom of Company "H" Marine Support Battalion, at Homestead Air Force Base, south of Miami, and near the Everglades of Florida. There were about 50 Marines on that base and just after arriving there, I, the junior man—a lance corporal—broke my hand and had to wear a cast which prevented me from properly performing my primary duties. Some of the guys remembered off hand there in the fall of 1968 were: the C.O., Captain P. Leonard; Gunny Don Brown; Gunny Weeks; Gunny Castle; SSgt Dave McWatters; SSgt Irons; Sgts Jerry Stephenson and Sam Brandsma; Cpl Jay Bloise; and LCpls Vince Baskovick, Gary Holmes, Tom Huddleston, and Don Lassiter.

I had to work in the company supply room because of the cast. After the whole room was squared away, Gunny Weeks told me to clean the two .30 Cal. Browning machine guns. I had never touched one before, but having a natural talent for mechanics I had, in short order, completely taken them all the way down, cleaned and reassembled them, although I couldn't get the bolt to go home all the way. The Gunny came in and was amazed. He had been a 0331 machine-gunner in Korea, and revealed to me the secret to getting the bolt home and seating a round; I had to back off the barrel 3 clicks to get the proper "headspace." After doing like he said, they worked just fine. That came in handy a few weeks later when we had a training exercise in the Everglades where I was the machine-gunner for the aggressors the whole exercise. One of the SNCOs took several pictures, and I was surprised when he handed me one of the photos a week or so later.

Me with a .30 cal. M/G during a training exercise in the Everglades in 1968 while at Co. "H" Marine Support Battalion.

Back to Vietnam. After a couple months at FSB Fuller, it was my turn to make a run for supplies back to Dong Ha combat base for more BBs (all Marines know that as beans, bullets and bandages, but for us it could have been batteries, beer and a bath. We had all the bullets we needed—courtesy of 2/4 Marines!). I caught an ARVN, UH-34D from FSB Fuller to Dong Ha, and when I walked into the 1st Radio Battalion Compound, I believe it was Capt. Carnako said something like, "Well, Sergeant Truitt, how are you doing?" That made me happy, because I was a corporal. I well remember the date as 13 December 1969, and the captain said, "Go on in the operations bunker and I'll get your warrant. Just as I walked in, the Gunny said, "Truitt, I need you to run up to the Vinh Dai Crusher and get me a fuse at the 3rd Tanks Battalion. You can take that Jeep over there, but you gotta get up there and get back as fast as you can." About that time, the captain showed up, promoted me to sergeant backdated to the 1st of December, handed me a metal sergeant's chevron for my cover, and I took off to the crusher as it was getting late.

Wasting no time, I quickly headed west on Hwy 9 by myself, and was just about to turn left into the crusher at dusk when I noticed a bunch of commotion by the entrance. Wow, that's gross: an M-48 tank had run completely over a M-151 Jeep. The whole Jeep was compressed into a block like you see in the movies; it would now fit between the tracks and the space from the ground to the undercarriage of the tank.

Instead of a "rock crusher," to me that place became a "Jeep crusher." I drove on in and up to the command bunker, and there was still a lot of commotion. There were lots of rounds being fired, and tracers—although I just saw red tracers at that time—and several loud explosions. As soon as my Jeep stopped, a Marine ran out and said, "We're having a sapper attack. Can you operate a .30 Cal. machine gun?" (I guess they had them rather than M-60s because they were indigenous to the M-48 tanks.) That Marine grabbed me by the shoulder and said, "Good! Get up on top of the bunker and I'll get you an A/gunner soon as I can." A couple of minutes later that Gunny climbed up with another Marine, a couple of boxes of belted rounds and

M-48 Tank

The Vinh Dai Jeep Crusher errr Rock Crusher—3rd Tanks Battalion & Sea Bees

a can of 30 weight motor oil. He told me, "You've got it. If it gets hot from shooting, just pour some of this here oil in the receiver and keep it working." He also told me to stay there until relieved, to shoot anything out past the wire or that came through, and that when I needed more ammo, there was plenty more in the bunker. I didn't see him again until the next morning, but my A/gunner did immediately go down and bring up a couple more cans of ammo. Also of interest, those 30 Cal M/Gs sure do put out one heck of a lot of white smoke when you pour a little oil on a hot gun. Well, it was an interesting night, and the next morning everything and everyone seemed to be intact, although one of the tanks had a hole in the turret from an RPG. I don't know if anybody was killed, but I headed back to Dong Ha with the fuse as soon as I could.

Upon arriving back at 1st RadBn, my target was the ops bunker with the fuse. Someone said, "Hey, it's Truitt. We thought you were dead. We just sent a message out saying that you were run over by a tank." Well, they immediately got another message out which kept Linda from having a Marine vehicle drive up to our trailer in South Florida to give her the news.

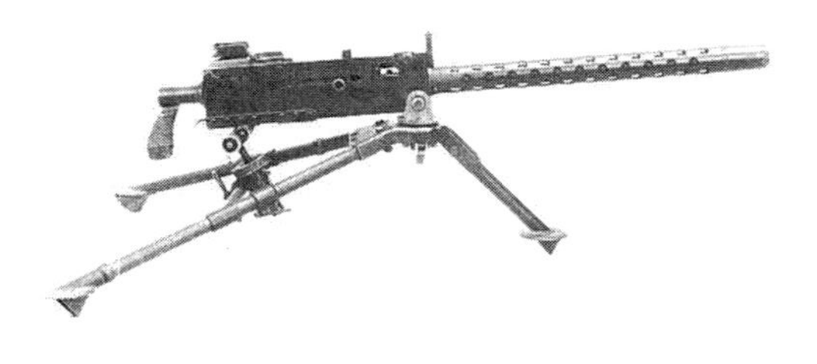

.30 Cal. M/G

After cleaning up, I caught a bird back up to FSB Fuller with another load of BBs. It was probably on that resupply run that the shower heater caught fire while I was taking a shower.

Seems like that little incident would have been qualification for a CAR. I had already qualified, however, on the 17th of November back at Fuller when the 246th NVA Regiment, supported by an NVA arty unit, tried to overrun us and make me start squirting "red stuff" (see the previous story). We sure put a big hurt on them, and they retreated back to the DMZ to regroup.

Di Dah, Di Da Dit

Sgt Truitt back in Dong Ha after manning the .30 M/G all night during a "sapper" attack.

18 Just Stomp 'Em, or Stick 'Em

"ALL STATIONS, ALL STATIONS; THIS IS FLORIDA VACATION, Alpha, with a message on Bravo Zulu! Stand by to receive traffic!" Yep, it's me, Echo-Five-Tango (Chuck Truitt), and my orders to move from FSB Fuller back to Dong Ha came just a couple days after going back up to Fuller. As a result of a PRC-25 conversation with SSgt Dave Carpenter, I was going to be running the Net Control, and someone else would be replacing me on the mountain there. I wasn't even starting to get "ripe"

"Battalion Heavies": Maj. Ed Brinkley, Capt. Geo. Carnako, LtCol. DM Hopkins, & Maj. Jim Hatch —Photo Courtesy of George Carnako

Sgt Rick Swan in a bunker with a NOD (night observation device) and the controls for all the claymore mines in that section.

yet, having just taken a shower on my last run for "BBs." Oh well, you gotta do, what you gotta do.

Dong Ha's pig pen set out right behind the ops bunker, and next to the machine gun bunker with the big NOD (night observation device). It was a serious pig pen; a person could walk around in there. Furthermore, it was completely enclosed all the way around with sandbags and dirt-filled wooden ammo boxes, and it had a tent covering too, as I recall. Not only that, but it was up off the ground with a rough plank floor. I even saw two rat traps, of the standard variety, which means they had rats! Did you think this was going to be a story about pigs?

Probably the most common rat bait in the whole country of Vietnam was C-ration peanut butter from one of those little tin cans. During the last few weeks at Fuller, I found out that those doggies didn't know what a "John Wayne" (portable can opener) was. So you are probably thinking, "How did they open their

C's?" Well, the answer to that was, they used a P-38. No, that's not an airplane. A P-38 and a John Wayne are, in fact, one and the same piece of essential equipment. They just go by two different nomenclatures.

So those traps in Dong Ha were baited with peanut butter. Every time I came in, they had been tripped, flipped over, moved around or in some way molested, but they just weren't sufficient to catch those big NVA rats. I had been toying with two different methods to catch them, one of which I had successfully used up on the mountain. But the .45, as well as the blasting caps, were out of the question there at Dong Ha. The first method involved cutting one end completely out of a can. Then a standard can opener was used to punch holes in several places around the outside of the can, at the end that was just cut out. When you straighten the curled tips to slant inward, it can be made in such a way that the rat will go in, but will not be able to back again because of the points slanting inward, kind of like a fish trap (which is what gave me the idea in the first place). Well, I baited it with C-ration tuna fish.

Sgt Tom Huddleston and "pig" (PRD-1).

This is a Christmas card sent home to Mom which I got from a vendor while in Dong Ha, 1969.

It was hilarious when those big rats went crazy with a can stuck on their head, and noisy too with their banging into stuff. I did lose a couple of them (I have no idea where they went), but generally you could just stomp them or stick them. There was no rat body count in Dong Ha, though I did get a few rats using that method in the short time that I was there.

Di Dah, Di Da Dit

19 LZ Snoopy USMC

After spending a two to three week hiatus from Fire Support Base Fuller working as DF Net Control back at Dong Ha, I had to go back up on Fuller again. Don't get me wrong—I was all for it, I wanted to go back—although being in the "rear with the gear" at Dong Ha Combat Base (if you could call that the rear!) definitely had its major benefits. It was certainly nice

Looking south from our ops bunker towards the 105mm arty area. There is an army "slick" about to come in on the purple smoke. Notice the baby-blue 105mm shell casings, just before they painted the LZ!

to spend the 1969 Christmas and New Year holidays in a place that had a real chow hall—well, kind of any-how—and that wonderful shower. Also, in Dong Ha I slept in a nice hard-back hootch, with a living area that was big enough to walk around in. A nice change. The guys had also made a hootch into a clubhouse (I guess you could call it that), and as I recall they had cold beverages available.

A freshly painted 105mm howitzer.

On Fuller, my home was a hole-in-the-ground bunker with dirt walls and floor, and a leaky PSP (runway matting) ceiling covered with sandbags, but I had really grown fond of that place. However, the Army's 1st of the 5th Mechanized Division had replaced the 4th Marines about November (the whole 3rd Marine Division was leaving Vietnam) which left just the few of us from 1st Radio Battalion as the only Marines there. Remember, the Marines took that position three different times before deciding to keep it manned. So FSB Fuller had a completely Marine heritage.

Just after the army arrived, they started bringing in can after can of paint. Those guys painted everything. For instance, all the engineer stakes around the LZ, as well as any others whose sharp end could injure someone, had a spent 105mm shell casing put over the end. I'll never forget, those doggies didn't like the bare brass of the shells so they painted every single one of those shell casings "baby blue" at our end of the FSB, and red at the artillery's end. Those folks were serious about it; they painted everything that didn't move for more than a day.

Well, after a little while they got bored, I guess, with nothing else to paint. I thought they would start painting the sandbags themselves, but no? They decided to paint the LZ. Yep, that's right, they painted the LZ. It was maybe about 50 foot square. There was a real artist there in the army, and that guy did a decent job of painting a big Snoopy sitting on his doghouse. Snoopy had his WW I fighter ace, leather helmet on, with his arms outstretched, holding a joystick that stuck up between his legs. Every bird, fixed wing, or otherwise in the whole northern "I" Corps area could see Snoopy, the WW I ace sitting on his dog house. Actually, it really did look great, but we Marines were a bit peeved.

On top of that mountain, we used to get really socked in there in the clouds. Sometimes we couldn't see anything. Well, I knew where their paint locker was (made out of ammo crates, the common building material. Our own Joe Armstrong could make anything out of an ammo crate). It was right close to the LZ and not far from our bunker. I went over to the LZ and, walking all over that thing, I laid out a plan in my head—to paint a great big, black USMC on the top of that yellow dog house. The joints in the PSP worked out just perfect to paint the big letters too. I then went back into our ops bunker, laid it all out on paper and talked it up to the other Marines. One of them was recruited to help.

Looking north from the 105mm howitzer emplacements after the army painted the shell casings red in this area, but baby blue on the other side of the LZ, closer to the flags.

After dark, and while we were still heavily socked in, we got two cans of black paint and brushes from the locker. The visibility was really bad but we crawled out onto the LZ and painted the "needed" addition. We could have been shot, but since we were inside the perimeter and almost everyone's attention was to the outside, we did okay. After just one interruption, we proceeded to finish the job about an hour later. Then we went and put the paint back as if absolutely nothing was different.

Wow! When the morning came, there was really a lot of "hate and discontent." I'm not sure, but my memory seems to tell me that I, a sergeant, was the senior Marine in the bunch ATT, for a couple days anyhow. Maybe SSgt. Joe Armstrong had left permanently, or was gone on a resupply run. Regardless, I

LZ "Snoopy," from an approaching "46" before the USMC addition.

was the man responsible and definitely the guy who was chewed on by the Army OIC, a captain. He said stuff like, "We try to make things nice, and you Marines always screw everything up." Actually, those soldiers had really been pretty decent to us, and we certainly got a lot of "bennies" from them.

The captain wanted me to go out and paint over the USMC, but I refused. I countered with something like, "It was the Marines who fought and died for this mountain, three times, and we haven't left yet. We're just letting you stay up here with us." Then he insisted on me getting our OIC on the PRC-25, which I did. After a little while he called me back on the "25" and said "Don't do anything; someone is coming up." Whoa, I thought I was in "deep kimchee," and waited with anticipation for the arrival of I didn't know who.

Well, it was either later that day or the next that it cleared up to be beautiful outside. I could hear a "Huey" approaching with

LZ Snoopy in the middle of FSB Fuller just after the army painted it. Courtesy of SgtMaj "Fighting Joe" Joe Armstrong

A UH-1E, Notice the MARINES on the side; it's a HUEY

a distinctive thump, thump, thump from the blades "breaking wind" as they cut the air. I heard it from way off and thought that this might be our anticipated visitor. As I watched the approach, a UH-1E—with USMC on the sides—began circling overhead. Ha! There were a couple people hanging out taking pictures. I walked on over to the LZ as the bird landed, and a Marine major with at least one other officer stepped down off the bird. In retrospect, I believe it was Major Robert O'Brien, the XO for 1st Radio Bn. in DaNang, who had come all of those miles just for this event. The major immediately started walking toward me with a great big smile on his face and his hand held way out in front to shake my hand.

Without a doubt, that was a huge show of support, as well as a big relief to my psyche. Our battalion headquarters was in DaNang and the rest of the 1st Radio Battalion was so spread to the winds from Chu Lai to the DMZ, that us DFers rarely ever saw our battalion's field grade officers. He was sure a sight for sore eyes that day. If I'm not mistaken, he is the same major that came out bringing gifts, such as a canned ham and a couple cases of beverage, and to be with us on 10 November 69—the Marine

Corps' birthday. He never said one bad word to me, and I was not spoken to again by that army captain either.

The last of us Marines ended up departing the mountain just a few weeks later in conjunction with the 3rd MarDiv leaving earlier. But I did create one more incident as we left FSB Fuller.

Di Dah, Di Da Dit

20 Awe and Wonder

DID YOU EVER SHOOT A .50 CALIBER MACHINE GUN? I HAVE, and they're like a big 30 cal. M/G. The traversing mechanism might be practically the same too; that's on the tripod that the gun sits on. The 30 cal. has a pistol grip handle and regular type trigger at the back end, whereas the 50 cal. has two hand grips with a butterfly lever that you can depress with either thumb.

A 50 cal is a big M/G and shoots a bullet that is one half inch in diameter—thus .50 caliber—which is also measured as 12.7mm for NATO-type people. A 50 cal is very effective against lightly armored vehicles, aircraft and of course, the "little people" (bad guys, gooks, slopes, NVA, zips, zipper heads and an assortment of other names for the enemy). The 30 cal is a bit smaller, more portable and easier to handle. They are effective against unarmored vehicles, aircraft and of course the "little people" as well. Its bullets are about 1/3 of an inch in diameter, also measured as 30-06 and @7.62mm.

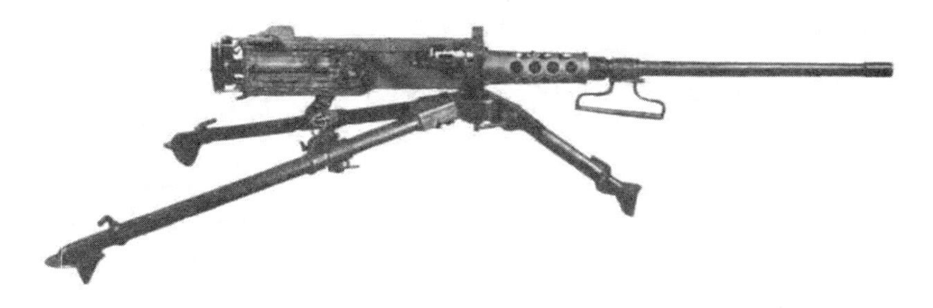

M2, 50 Caliber Machine Gun

A couple UC123 aircraft spraying Agent Orange.

In the fall of 1969, we were clearing out trees at Fire Support Base (FSB) Fuller to provide more clear area past our barbed wire. That way we'd be able to see the "little people" better if they should foolishly decide to hit us (while the Marines were manning the place). We had laboriously worked out and cleared overlapping fields of fire to give a warm welcome to any undesired visitors. Clearing fields of fire was always interesting. We had no heavy equipment but some of those trees were huge. Now the Air Force came in and defoliated the place by spraying Agent Orange several times and the trees were bare, but they still needed to be cut down.

(Let me digress here. My daughter was born about six months before I went to Nam. When I returned, my wife Linda, my two-year old daughter Marie and I went to Scotland for a three-year tour. While there, Linda and I really wanted to increase the size of our family, but the only result was miscarriages. Come to find out, as per a recent pamphlet from the VA, Agent Orange was the cause of many wives having miscarriages rather than full-term pregnancies. Evidently, my exposure to the high concentration of Agent Orange there on Dong Ha mountain for those several months in 1969 and 1970 is what caused us to be limited to such a small family.)

Back to FSB Fuller: Just fooling around, I fired a LAAW (light anti-tank assault weapon) 66mm rocket into a tree which made a real big noise and shook the tree tremendously, knocking down a bunch of branches and twigs, but all it really did was punch a hole all the way through the tree. Well, it was fun, but it sure didn't do much except help the woodpeckers and impress the rock-apes.

I want to point out something I think is interesting. I have given several classes on the proper operation of a LAAW to the Marines. Later, I came to realize that the same weapon was used by the U.S. Army, but they called it a LAWs rocket, not using the double "AA." The weapons I used and taught had a label right on the thing that said LAAW.

One of the effective ways that we used to cut down trees was to shoot them down with a 50 cal M/G. By aiming first at one side of the tree and squeezing off a round, then turning a couple clicks on the traversing mechanism (which moved the aim of the barrel further across the tree) and firing another round, some of those big trees would come tumbling down in just a little while.

Quan, Armstrong and Sen —Courtesy of Joe Armstrong

This brings me to the finer subject of using C4 to blow up the trees. This is an interesting subject: C4 is super fun to play with. Seems like it's white or real pale yellow and normally comes in 1.25 pound bars, very much like modeling clay. You can shape it into cars, birds, rabbits, toy soldiers or just about anything, and then blow them to smithereens when you're all done. They are also great for heating up a helmet full of water or liquid food. With a thumb-sized ball, just roll it around in the dirt real good, with an emphasis on lots of dirt so that it will burn more slowly, and then light the thing. It may be hard to light, but when it starts burning it'll be real hot and heat up what's needed fast.

Seems like it was an ongoing project, to clear and extend our fields of fire. Even after the 3rd Mar Div left the "I" Corps area and the Army's 1st of the 5th Mech took over, they got into the act. The only way I ever saw them do it, though, was by blowing trees with C4. Another Marine and I were watching some doggies go through the wire at the north end to blow some of those huge trees that were outside the wire. They'd tie some sticks of C4 around the tree with "det cord" (it looks like a plastic clothesline filled with C4) and set the fuse for about 15 minutes. Then they worked their way back up and over the sandbagged wall to await the boom. Sometimes the trees would go down, but often it would take a second demo shoot as there was just a big inverted donut around those bigger trees after just one shoot.

I don't recall which Marine it was that helped me, but after watching those doggies we decided to go and show 'em how it should be done. After talking to them, they said "Sure, have at it," which we did. We went down with plenty of C4 and the determination to blow some big trees. The doggies went completely back up the side of the mountain, and we proceeded to prepare a "big one." Since those doggies were just tying the C4 on the trees with that "det cord," we decided we were going to

Looking northwest towards Mutter's Ridge, Hill 484, and the DMZ.

do the job right. So we laid the explosive around the base of the tree and packed it in with big rocks. Then we cut about 15 minutes of fuse and proceeded back up and over the wall to await the boom.

KA-WHAMMMM, and the tree lifted up like a rocket taking off, but all of those rocks that we had packed over the C4 turned into many, many smaller rocks and some of them must have gone a couple thousand feet into the air. Well, none of us got hit, but for sure it rained rocks that day. However, just one time only! It's not that we Marines made a mistake, it's just that after that we sought a less impressive technique to fill those soldiers with awe and wonder.

Di Dah, Di Da Dit

21 Pop a Yellow Smoke

I GOTTA TELL YOU ALL THIS STORY, AND I DO IT WITH SOME ambivalence. Let me explain. Ever since I wrote the story "LZ Snoopy USMC," I've been anticipating writing this one, but it takes me a long time to write even a short one. I have to sit and think and remember; after all it has been 33 years. As I'm writing, often I'll remember something else—a little tidbit—and then I'll have to go back and amend what I've already written. As I think about it, sometimes I just start chuckling to myself, or even laughing out loud because, to me, it was very a funny experience. But, on the other hand, today at a much more mellow 53 years old, and I believe more considerate of other folks, even doggies (one of my best friends is an army sergeant major) there is in me something that says "Chuck, that was not nice!" Ha, Ha, Hmmm.

Just a few weeks after the modification of the Snoopy doghouse incident, which would have put it right around the end of January 1970, all of the 1st Radio Battalion was moving operations further south, closer to DaNang. We got the word up there on FSB Fuller that we would also be relocated.

After the 4th Marines left, and the few of us 1st Radio Battalion guys were still up there, things were a lot different. Those combat veteran Marines were replaced by a company of soldiers that, according to what they told me, had four combat veteran NCOs and the rest were green, just recently in-country men. It must have gotten better later on, but it was a bit scary at

A soldier drops an 81mm "Lume" down the tube to seat the base plate. I understand that an enemy round hit this mortar pit several months after we left. It caused a large secondary explosion that took out the whole mortar pit as well as most of what had been our operations bunker, and 33 ARVN soldiers were killed.

first. I'll never forget one M-16 (one of the newer ones with the round flash suppresser, not the three-pronged ones like we had) lay up against the sandbagged wall for three days and got a red film on it before it was ever moved.

Those army medics had 45s, brand new ones. Mine was shot out; the lands and grooves were just about gone. I had gotten a case of 45 tracer ammo, which wasn't in a normal ammo can; it was a big green can holding 800 rounds, and it opened on the end with a key, just like opening an old coffee can or sardine can. I suppose they used those 45 tracers in the old "grease guns" and probably "Tommy guns." I used to shoot at a 55 gallon drum on the ridge 350 meters to the west of us. Bracing the pistol on the sandbags, I'd fire towards the ridge, using a lot of "Kentucky windage" and watch those tracers burn in a big basketball-like arc towards the drum. My barrel was so shot out that I couldn't even hit a beer can thrown just outside the sandbagged wall. Even by bracing the pistol with sandbags, still the dirt would kick up all around the can. Seriously, the lands and grooves looked more like dimples. Well, the army helped me out with that. All those medics carried a 45. In the bunker just down from us was a medic who always left his pistol belt hanging from a table just inside his bunker. I got one of my other Marines to sidetrack the medic while I did a quick field strip of his pistol and switched barrels on him. WOW, what a difference. I could now see dirt kicking up around the drum over there on the ridge 350 yards away and occasionally hit the thing with a perceptible bang, even at that range.

It is 350 meters to the bare spot on that ridge just west of us.

I really liked it up there on Fuller, and I felt that I was really effective in my part of the war. There were a lot of NVA, and VC too, who were put out of action because of us 1st RadBn SigInt/EW guys. Yes, that seems like a pretty cosmetic/euphemistic way of saying it. Since I worked DF—which was actively involved in locating the enemy—and I was told that our equipment was designed for up to 12 miles, you can understand that we had to be very near the enemy to be effective. Well, we were, and it was.

Net control would send us coordinates when we had a fix on a location. A fix with a CEP (circular error of probability) of a 1000 meters to me was junk, although valuable in knowing the general area of a particular enemy unit. Often we'd get 300 meter or less fixes, and sometimes 100 meter fixes on the "bad guys." But, remember this was 33 years ago, though I do remember things pretty good from that time.

The army took over the six 105mm howitzers, and one day the army arty OIC, a mustang lieutenant, if I recall, came in and talked to me since I was the DF dude. He told me that he had formerly worked with the ASA (Army Security Agency) and knew all about what we did, and especially knew about the pigs (PRD-1s) and their capabilities. He told me that I could walk right in to his bunker, stick a pin in the map and not tell him anything, but just make sure it was a 300 meter fix or less, and he could have steel on the target "Most Ricky Tick." Now you have to understand that they had info on our own and ARVN operations and positions, so he knew where not to lay in a fire mission but, on more than one occasion, I'd stick the map and almost immediately there was a fire mission and a splash on target real fast. Mutters Ridge, just a thousand meters north, was the splash area on several occasions as I recall, as was the Razorback to the west. There was a ridge just to our NE, between us and A4, that I recall putting steel on as well; that's the same ridge where I saw two birds (Cobras) get shot down on in one day—seems like near the end of January 1970—just before we left.

I sure hated to leave that place. I remember on two occasions Bn Hqs sent us an SP pack (sundry pack) which is supposed to be for a hundred men. There were usually only five or six of us, plus our two "dancers." An SP pack was a box of goodies like razors and blades, not that we had much use for them up there since we just had drinking and cooking water. There were also cards, soap, cigarettes and chewing tobacco, as well as an assortment of candy and other things. Now most of that stuff was useless to us, but it made great trading material! With the SP stuff, we got LRPs (long range patrol rations), cans of dehydrated beef patties, canned donut mix and cooking oil, plus a bunch of other

An Army 105mm howitzer at Fuller, with its pretty red trim.

You can always tell a burning helicopter by the thick black smoke.

really good stuff—all from those soldiers. I even traded for one of their metal framed rucksacks and one of their soft flack jackets. I got rid of that plated piece of junk, flack jacket that the Marines were stuck with. That also made it nicer firing the 40mm M-79, which kicked like a mule when firing the shotgun rounds, although the HE was okay.

While filling sandbags and working at Vandergrift Combat Base in August, I started putting a pebble in my mouth and rolling it around to keep my mouth from drying out so bad in the heat. Boy, that's tough sometimes when you turn your head fast or make some other movement. It can make you see stars when you bite down on one of those pebbles. That's why and when I first started chewing tobacco. I'd get Redman and Days Work there at Stud, but on FSB Fuller, those SP packs had Mail Pouch—pretty good, Beechnut—yuck, and Redman—oorah! I chewed tobacco from August 1969 until January 1981. That's a tough thing to stop, and I love that Redman. I just don't chew it anymore. Poor Linda, I suppose it sure made for some embarrassing times for that dear lady. Not only that, it's embarrassing sometimes with those brown streaks down the side of the car when a spit didn't go as well as planned. Linda used to hate to drive with the brown streaks; I do remember washing them off a few times for her. It's been a long time now, praise the Lord!

Man, I forgot where I was at. Oh yeah! Leaving Fuller, Ha! Seems like we already had most of the gear that we were taking staged by the LZ when the four of us left. We were awaiting a Huey to pick us up. Oh, you do know that the Marine version of a UH-1E was called a Huey, but the doggies had a slightly different version (I've been on all of them, plus others too) of UH-1 which they called a Slick. They're not the same! Did you ever wonder why a Marine UH-1E is called a Huey? Well, try and phonetically pronounce UH-1E; it comes out kinda like "Huey!"

To get to the army's command post bunker, where the captain stayed most of the time, it was a straight shot. From the LZ to the CP you had to go north about 40 to 50 yards, just up and over the highest point of the fire base and down a little, right near the northern end. So from the LZ you could run the 50 yards north, up over the top, then right over and across that command bunker and right on down to the northern perimeter

This is a Marine Corps Huey—UH-1E!

wall. On the top of their bunker was the end of a wooden ammo crate sticking up with the ends taken out. It went right down into the bunker as a chimney, or vent hole. You could actually talk right down into that bunker through the end of that ammo crate vent. It only stuck up a few inches higher than all the thousands of sandbags around it. Well, on the spur of the moment, I got a great idea.

As soon as we threw our gear into the Huey, I yelled to the pilot, "Wait a minute, I forgot something." He gave me the "high sign" so I grabbed a yellow smoke grenade and took off running up over the top, while the bird sat on the LZ with the blades turning. In a flash I pulled the pin but kept my hand over the spoon. As soon as I got to the vent, I released the spoon, "pii-inggg" dropped the smoke down the vent and took off back to the LZ. Never missing a step I flew into that Huey and yelled "Go, Go, Go!" Now I have to tell you, there was one other Marine standing next to the bird waiting for me to come back, and when I jumped aboard, he then boarded, being the last

One of our dancers atop a bunker. —Courtesy of Rob Charnell

Marine on Fuller. I didn't want to argue with him, I just wanted that bird to "didi mau."

As the bird was climbing up and around the north end of Fuller, I looked out to see an extremely interesting sight. As I'm remembering this and putting it down on paper, I'm absolutely cracking up. I can hardly type properly, and I've got water sprinkles on the inside of my glasses. (Now if you're in the army, it's because I'm crying in remorse. But, if you know me, or you're in the Marines, I'm really hurting because my sides are splitting at the remembrance of it all.) In my mind's eye I'm watching billows of yellow smoke come out of the entrance of that bunker, and from up out of the vent. There are three soldiers sprawled on the sandbagged surface in front, with yellow smoke curls all around them, and one more soldier bursting through the entrance way, then rolling out across the sandbags. The Marines finally let the army have the whole mountain all to themselves.

Yes, 33 years later, I've got mixed emotions. I'd never do anything like that today, but it sure is funny to remember!

Di Dah, Di Da Dit

22 Watch Him

"Roger that! Echo five tango, out." I had gotten the word that we were moving down to DaNang and 1st Radio Battalion Headquarters. This was all happening at the end of January or the first part of February 1970. From Bn. Hqs. we'd be split up and sent "to the winds"; that is, to wherever we were needed individually. Of course, that was the nature of the work that my MOS (military occupational specialty) did. We were usually sent out and attached to, or worked closely with, some other combat unit. I had worked with the 4th Marine Regiment at Vandergrift Combat Base and on Dong Ha mountain, except

1stRadBn barracks, Camp Horn, DaNang—Tuttle & Williams. —Courtesy of Gary Williams

for the past few weeks when it was with the doggies of the 1st Brigade of the 5th Mechanized Division. This shift further south and away from the DMZ was in conjunction with the 3rd Marine Division permanently leaving Vietnam. It's my understanding that since I had been in-country just under six months, I got to stay. Looking back on it though, I think that probably no one from 1st RadBn would be included in that six month ruling.

Everything I owned was on my back. I got a C-123 "Provider" out of Dong Ha and went to Battalion Hqs. at DaNang for several days while they figured out what to do with me. Now let me tell you, I was really leery of riding in the back of that "Provider." They had proven to be great aircraft over the years, and they were used for about every kind of mundane job the military could come up with in the transportation category. This particular aircraft that flew a "milk run" between Danang and Dong Ha was in pretty rickety shape. It wouldn't even hold pressurization due to the shrapnel and bullet holes. There were no seats, not even web seats. Everyone just got in and sat on big metal pallets that covered the whole floor, with nylon straps from side to side as a seat belt for the whole bunch in that row.

The whole problem for me was that the last time I flew on one of these things, I almost lost the ends of my fingers on both hands. I had been sitting down cross-legged on the thin metal pallet with the edge just behind me. My arms were out behind bracing me, with my hands on the floor/pallet and my fingers curling over the edge. There was a space of an inch or two before the leading edge of the next pallet behind. As we were about to land, I moved my hands to grasp the tether across my lap. As the plane touched down (must have been a Marine pilot who had recently been landing on a carrier), all the pallets shifted forward and that gap between the pallets closed with a loud smack. I'm sure glad that my fingers were no longer there, and I definitely made the crew chief aware of the potential hazard. With all those

1st Radio Battalion Headquarters, DaNang, RVN. —Courtesy of Rob Charnell

folks (both Vietnamese civilians and American military) who flew on that plane, I have wondered all these years if anyone was ever hurt from such a hazard.

"Sgt. Truitt, you're going to An Hoa to work with 1st RadBn's 1st Platoon, and you'll be going down in that 6-by over there." I have a couple recollections of my trip that day, as I rode in the back of the truck to An Hoa. I remember heading SW out of DaNang and seeing Hill 55 sticking up to our left and Hill 10 on the right. Somewhere between there and the river was a village that would play a marked role in one incident of my life a few months later. Also in that general vicinity was Hill 37 where 1st Rag Bag had a platoon at an old French bunker, although I never went into their compound.

Still moving south we came to the river, and crossing the river was Liberty Bridge. After leaving the Liberty Bridge area, the road proceeded south to An Hoa (5th Marines TAOR) and the Que Son mountains on beyond (that was the 7th Marines TAOR after about August 1969). I think I'd rather operate with the 5th Marines and in their primary nemesis, the Arizona Territory, than the 7th Marines who had to traipse through the mountains. Humping those hills would be the pits, as if the rice paddies, rice paddy dikes and the nasty tree lines of the 5th Marines were a "walk in the park."

Before pulling into An Hoa, we made a short stop at Hill 10. No, it's the other Hill 10, the little knoll just outside of An Hoa. It was nothing, I mean "whoop-de-do," this place was just a bump alongside the road south. I got out of the PC (truck) and looked around a bit. Seems like there was a hole in the ground with a pig antenna sticking up, that was about the highest thing. Everything here was at ground level. Everyone lived in holes covered with poncho liners (it reminded me of a community of ground hogs). Concertina wire was strung around the whole place but nothing above ground, nothing at all. There was a big hole where the little people blasted in a lob bomb the night before. No one was hurt though. I guess it was lobbed in from a hundred yards or so outside of the wire. (A lob bomb is a piece of unexploded ordinance, usually a 100 or 250 pound aerial bomb dud that is rearmed and hand carried to its launch point where a charge of some kind is used to lob the ordinance on to its target a short distance away. They are very inaccurate, but capable of creating beaucoup "hate and discontent" if they by

An Hoa with the Que Son mountains in back, at the end of monsoon season.

chance land on or near something. Well, we didn't stay long, just long enough to drop off some supplies to our RadBn personnel, of which there were two. I believe Hill 10 was an OP of 2/5 Marines.

There was just a little ways yet to An Hoa, and we approached it from the east. Off to the south side of the road as we entered An Hoa, I could see the concrete and steel skeletons of buildings from an old factory, evidently in its heyday during French Colonial rule. What really sticks in my mind about entering An Hoa was the big open field that we drove across as we entered. Because the monsoons were nearly finished, the whole field was covered with a layer of water several inches deep—dark red muddy water from the red earth that was there. As we drove across the field, the tires created a red wave that proceeded out from the 6-by and eventually crashed on the shores at the farthest limits of the big field. About two months later I was coming back from a resupply run to DaNang with Top Fitzgerald in a PC vehicle, and as we came upon the open field about to enter An Hoa Combat Base we saw a CH53-A, Sea Stallion helicopter hovering near the far end of the field at about 30 to 40 feet. The field was dried up and the red mud had turned to a very fine, red talcum powder.

The other Hill 10, between An Hoa and Liberty Bridge

That dust was swirling and circulating in an amazing thick red cloud through those chopper blades. It was quite an impressive site. That red dust settled everywhere and permeated everything. I'll bet the air crew was really hating it.

Upon entering the outer perimeter of An Hoa from the east, we had to traverse through the 2nd Battalion, 5th Marine Regiment (2/5 Marines) area first, then through part of 3/5's area before arriving at the 1st Platoon, 1st RadBn bunker. Right next door was the 5th Marines S2 bunker (regimental intelligence) that we were attached to, or at least working very closely with. I remember my mailing return address was: Hq Co, 5th Marines, S2 (RB), FPO San Francisco, 96602. The southern perimeter of the base wasn't very far, but it was a few hundred yards to the eastern perimeter. A little east and near the southern perimeter was that big tower with the RPG net in front of it. Almost underneath that tower was where my first abode would be—a PC tent I had all to myself. There were several hardback hootches all around, but my tent was right in the middle of a small clearing, all by itself; but not yet!

Looking east from our ops bunker in An Hoa.

An Hoa tower and RPG net, from about where the PC tent was at.

When I reported inside our Ops bunker, I was immediately chewed upon by one totally grouchy gunnery sergeant, Max Kerr. "Sgt. Truitt, you are a dirt bag" (that's not really what he said, but I don't want to write it down here). "Well, great gobs of gravy, guns, I just got a shower in DaNang before coming down here. I haven't even had time to sweat this crud out of my pores yet." Woe, woe, woe, let me tell you something folks, if you ever meet up with Gunny Max Kerr, DO NOT, I say again, DO NOT call him 'Guns,' even if he is a gunnery sergeant. "Sgt. Truitt, don't unpack! Get your gear and get over to the LZ. You're going to Hill 65. They've got a corporal and a lance corporal there who are linguists. They are using a KY-38 with an encryption key, KYK-38. That new secret radio has to have a sergeant watching it, and you are the sergeant that's gonna watch it. The only thing you have to do is protect that radio and change the key settings each day. Don't screw up!" Whew, I musta had bad breath or something!

Needless to say, I abruptly found myself at the LZ where I caught a CH-53A back northwest a little ways to Hill 65, right next to Charlie Ridge. The Gunny told me to wait by the Hill 65 LZ till one of the guys came down and showed me where the 1st Rag Bag hootch was. 1st Radio Bn didn't have a bunker there, just a hootch with dirt-filled ammo boxes that made up about four to five feet of the sides all the way around. So I waited, and waited; the Gunny must've forgot to radio ahead that I was coming. So, I carried everything I owned under a lean-to waiting area in the shade—a doggies metal-framed ruckpack, with one pair of cammies, and an extra pair of boots, my M-79 with one claymore bag of HE rounds, a .45 Auto w/ 200 rounds and 4 magazines, my T/O M-16 and two bandoleers of magazines with 18 rounds in each mag. I was loaded for bear and there would never again be an opportunity to use either the .45 or the

Terry Wheeler, Unk, Bob Raz, Steve Lehman —Courtesy of Steve Lehmann

M-79. Gone were the good times; now all that stuff was just useless baggage!

While I waited to be picked up, I saw a very interesting sight. There under the cover of the lean-to was a big dog and his handler, a corporal, who were watching a captured Viet Cong. He sure was a little guy, just waiting in that funny squatting position; he wasn't even tied up. The Marine was waiting for a bird to take the VC to DaNang, and the dog was resting at the handler's feet. That corporal said to me, "Check this out," then he said two words to the dog: "Watch him." Immediately the dog came alive and was right in front of that VC, face to face, and about four inches apart. That dog didn't move at all, and I guarantee you, that VC didn't flex a muscle, not even a little bit. Well, I was definitely impressed, and that "zipper head" appeared to be rather impressed too, in a funny sort of way. The corporal walked out into the open and smoked a cigarette; neither the dog nor the gook moved at all. I'm absolutely sure the dog could have devoured that little guy in no time, and still had dinner as a chaser.

In a little while, my guide finally showed up, walking!

DI DAH, DI DA DIT

23 Of Snake, Nape, and Stickmen

THERE SURE WAS A LOT OF KILLING GOING ON AT HILL 65 IN the spring of 1970. Most of the killing though was just flies, mosquitos and plain ol' time, with a big emphasis on the killing of time. After spending several months in the very northern "I" Corps area where things were often hopping and very interesting (mainly due to my active participation), now the whole world seemed to be moving in a slow, low crawl's pace. You have to understand that 1st Radio Battalion had about the same number of men as they had just a couple months before, but we were no longer supporting the 3rd Marine Division with intelligence, because they had left Vietnam and moved to Okinawa. Now we were just basically supplying intelligence for the 1st Marine Division because the Army's 1st Brigade of the 5th Mechanized Division had their own ASA elements that had taken over our jobs near the DMZ.

Many of us who had had important and useful jobs before were now scrounging for something to do because all the good jobs in support of the 1st Marine Division were already taken. I

A4 Airstrike—Napalm—just NE and outside of Hill 65.

LCpl Dusty Rhodes and Cpl Joe "Gags" Gagliano at the entrance to our hootch.

was capable of doing several things, but my specialty had been direction finding using my CW Morse code abilities.

The whole problem was that all the positions in the 1st Mar Div TAOR were already filled. There I was, a sergeant, babysitting a secret voice enciphering radio with a lance corporal and a corporal who had meaningful jobs using their Vietnamese linguistic abilities. I was bored stiff.

So there I was, stuck at Hill 65 south of DaNang. The prime reason for having a fire support base at Hill 65 was to help support the 5th Marine Regiment in its operations. It was within easy striking distance for targets in the Arizona Territory to the south and southwest, and towards Charlie Ridge to the west and northwest, all of which was the TAOR of the 5th Marines. The 11th Marine Regiment, an artillery regiment, is the 1st MarDiv's artillery regiment. For the 5th

An AH1 Cobra passing overhead

Marine Regiment (infantry), their artillery support was provided by the 11th Marine's 2nd Battalion, or 2/11, at An Hoa and Hill 65.

Because that FSB was there and already manned, 1st Radio Battalion used the resource to increase its support and coverage of the area with the two highly capable linguists, Gags and Dusty. Man, I felt like a sore thumb. Surely, they could find a better use for a sergeant than just watching a secret radio. I was there about six weeks. But in that six weeks not only did I get to watch the radio, I also watched several air strikes from A4 Skyhawks and the fabulous F4 Phantoms. Additionally, I saw for the first time A1 Skyraiders working out. They were impressive prop jobs with large clusters of bombs slung under the wings. Time after time after time, those "Spads," as they were called, would make runs dropping both Snake and Nape (Snake-Eye 250 lb HE bombs,) and 500-pound napalm bombs.

I'd usually go up on the roof and just sit or lie under the stars in the coolness of the evening. Often during the evening there was an artillery show. Very often there were illumination rounds (lume) being fired out, either from the big guns or the 81s. Almost any given night something was happening somewhere within sight, and we weren't too socked in to see it there either. Best of all, bad guys weren't shooting at us!

Here's an USAF A-1H SkyRaider w/lots of rockets, 2.75mm & Zuni—(special load). Most of the A-1s I saw were navy or Marine, white in color, w/lots of bombs & Zuni rockets.
—Courtesy of LtCol. Byron E. Hukee, USAF

"Nightwatch"—81mm Illumination flares "lume"

There was a never-ending assortment of aircraft transiting day and night; helicopters and fixed wing both were continually overhead. I'll never forget the day a big bird of some type was hauling an army M113 amtrack on an external load. It appeared to be coming from DaNang when it passed directly overhead at about 3000 feet or so. After it passed by, heading south across the river towards the Arizona Territory, all of a sudden I could see that track release from the bird and start falling, falling, falling, falling splat, and a big pall of dirt and dust ascended into the air. I've wondered at that many times over the years—if the helicopter was having some sort of trouble? Or,

Hill 65—the arrow points to approximate location of 1st Radio Battalion's unit.

One of several showers on Hill 65.

maybe the pilot inadvertently hit the release button. I wonder if the pilot said "Oops!" when he hit the button. I wondered if it landed in a village, or possibly on someone's house. If so, I bet they were surprised.

Our hootch was not like any of the ones I had been in yet. This one was quite roomy—about 20 foot square—and there were only three of us. The walls were not just plywood sheets like at Dong Ha and An Hoa, but were made from dirt-filled ammo boxes all the way around, with the only entrance at the center of the south end and a blast wall in front of that. Not only that, but there was a nearby shower. Wonderful! Hill 65 was 65 meters high, thus its name, and stuck up about 150 feet from the surrounding rice paddies. I understand that it was later called FSB Rawhide by the doggies. Hill 65 was shaped like an upside-down check, with the base at the north and the long side pointing southerly towards the Arizona Territory which was across the Song Vu Gia river.

A couple weeks before I left Hill 65, the 1st Rag Bag sent a DF team out to be with us. Man, that made me envious. Those guys already had the job before my being relocated from up north. Tom Huddleston had been stationed with me previously at Company "H" Marine Support Battalion in Florida. I hadn't seen him since then. I sure liked Tom. He was later wounded when an AK-47 round struck his helmet and rattled his "brain housing group."

Just a few days before leaving, there was quite a stir one day when several hundred people in what appeared to be black clad pajamas were spotted heading right straight towards the hill from the west at Charlie Ridge. I could see them all heading right toward us through my newly acquired 8x30 Canon binoculars someone had picked up for me from the PX in DaNang. That was a good set, and I still have them though they are a little smoky nowadays. Anyhow, we kept watching them advance from the stony ground on Charlie Ridge toward our position. Why weren't we plastering them with air and arty? Were we just letting them get closer and closer to spring some kind of trap? What was the deal? Finally, I could see through my binos, what those in charge must've seen earlier ago. That great horde of black pajama clad warriors was a whole community that had spent the day gathering firewood up on the Ridge. Each dark-clad villager was carrying two large stacks or ricks of sticks—one at each end of a pole that was being carried across his shoulders. Because the ricks were in an

Sergeant Tom Huddleston and Gags

upright position, and the carriers were somewhat hunched from the weight, each person appeared to be three. I guess you could call that a "force multiplier." Man, if we would have opened up on them, there'd have been sticks and stones and bones flying everywhere. That was sure quite a stir, and I can still see them coming 33 years later.

Di Dah, Di Da Dit

24 Bara Bara

Before I was ever sent to Vietnam, the Marine Corps sent me through a lot of training. My very first school after infantry training was at the Naval Communications Training Center, NCTC, Pensacola, Florida. It was the first few days of January 1968, and one memory that will always reverberate in my "brain housing group" is the Big Room and my introduction to Morse code. We sat there in front of an Underwood typewriter and a very skinny little 1st Class Petty Officer (I think his name was Lee), and another stocky, bald 1st Class (whose name was Sage) would yell out "Dit Dah," and we'd all answer back "Alpha" and strike the "A" key on the typewriter. For two weeks we did that till we got through the whole alphabet. It was a very nerve-wracking school, and it was finally over for me in August. There were about 400 Marines, and a whole bunch of squids (sailors) going through that school. I could write a book about my time there, but one memory is of Joe Schmuckatelli who was in my same squad bay, and we became friends. Joe was always talking about his girlfriend Barbara. Joe went downtown one weekend, and the next time I saw him he was sporting a pretty tattoo of a big red heart with an arrow going through it. He asked me how I liked it. I looked at it closer and started laughing. "Heh heh, Joe, I didn't realize your girlfriend's name was Barabara! Hey everybody, lookie here, you gotta see this!" The only tattoo artist in Pensacola at that time was about 85 years old and he had misspelled Barbara. From then on Joe

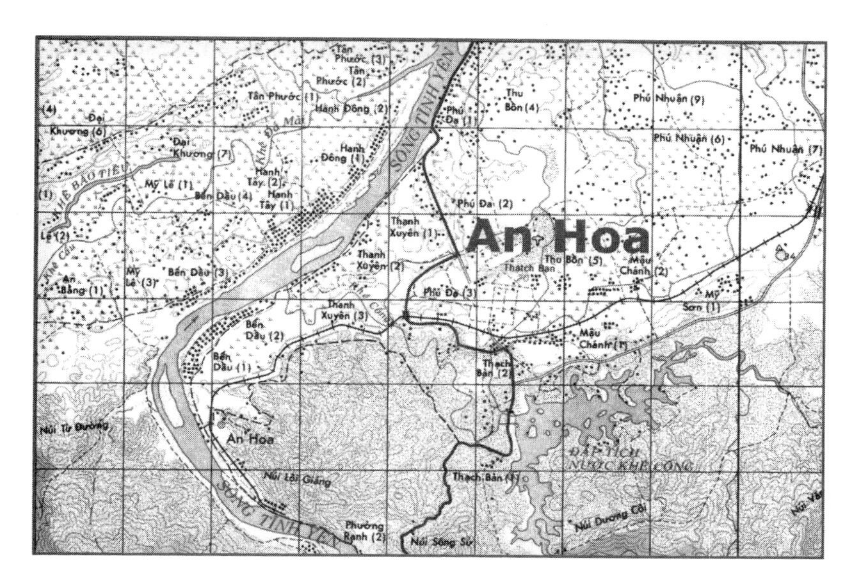

Schmuckatelli became known by everyone as BaraBara. Because his top secret clearance was later denied for some reason, BaraBara was sent to Camp Lejeune to become a 2531, field radio operator.

About two years later in Vietnam, my last view of Hill 65 was out of the back of a CH-53A as we spiraled up from the LZ, gaining altitude, ever higher over the hill so that we didn't receive any enemy fire. At two to three thousand feet we turned southeast and headed along the Song Vu Gia river and then southwest along the Song Tinh Yen towards An Hoa Combat Base, the regimental headquarters of the 5th Marine Regiment. An Hoa would be my home for the rest of my tour down south. That particular flight was interesting because I got a good birds-eye view of the Arizona Territory and an island in the middle of the river called Football Island. Numerous times over the years an incident involving that little island, a few weeks later, has protruded into my mind.

Upon setting down on the runway at An Hoa, the platoon's PC vehicle was there waiting to pick up my junk and me. Whoa, had something happened to change things since my last arrival at 1st Radio Battalion's 1st Platoon.

It was probably around the third week of March 1970, and things would be really different for the rest of my time in Vietnam. My first abode at An Hoa was a PC tent all by myself in the shadow of that big tower with the RPG net near the southern perimeter.

I don't remember exactly whether Gunny Kerr was just leaving or he had already left, but the new senior enlisted man was Master Sergeant Harry Fitzgerald. I'll never forget "The Top," he was a great guy. "Truitt, we just lost a couple guys who rotated back to the States and we need someone to maintain our generators. Can you do that?" "Sure, no sweat, Top, I've got a PU 239 license and I did that out at Vandergrift Combat Base; I can handle it." So, being the "generator guy" once again was one of my extra hats, but my primary hat was now communications security (ComSec). This time I didn't have the Greek to help me

Looking west from An Hoa Combat Base into the Arizona Territory. The arrow points to the approximate location of 1st Radio Battalion' 1st Platoon.

out as he found himself at Hill 37 further north and closer to DaNang. I went by Hill 37 several times; yes, that's exactly what I did, I went right on by and never went into the compound. A new lance corporal had just arrived from the States, so I trained him on the generators.

Just a day or two after my return to An Hoa, a McDonald's hamburger bag with about a dozen plain hamburgers in it arrived from one of the guys who had recently rotated. He posted it the first chance he had upon his return to The World (America). It was just a plain McDonald's bag that had been taped all the way around and labeled something like 1st Platoon, 1st Rad Bn, Headquarters-S2, 5th Marines, FPO San Francisco, Cal. 96602. All the hamburgers were immediately and completely eaten with gusto. They were probably the most enjoyed and appreciated several day-old hamburgers ever eaten in the history of the world.

Entrance to 1st RadBn's Operations bunker. —Courtesy of Rob Charnell

The ComSec mission required me to monitor communications from our own units in order to listen for mistakes that would inadvertently give information to the enemy, such as locations of units, future plans or some other info that would tip the bad guys off in some way. I was the only person who did that in the whole 5th Marines TAOR. Talk about being undermanned. I'd listen to the different radio nets on the different frequencies, and after about ten minutes on the job I realized that our whole communications security was a joke. Any enemy with just the slightest effort could get a wealth of information from us. Probably, a large percentage of our total losses in Vietnam were due to such poor communications discipline. So many radio operators had little-to-no procedural training that it was a real problem. Another problem was that every night what was called the BS net would become active. Guys would run their AN/PRC-25 (the common radio/telephone, short-range, voice radio) up to the highest frequency of 75.95 mhz and just "shoot

Sgt Truitt working ComSec, @ March, 1970.

the breeze" as if they were impervious to any enemy listening in. Guys would go by the most despicable call sign they could think of, and then proceed to talk about every sort of thing, including their mother's maiden name, and their sister's—oh, well, you get the idea.

One day I was monitoring an AH-1 Cobra Gunship, just north of us, flying along the Song Vu Gia towards Football Island. The pilot was desperately trying to get permission to fire on a sampan that had a bunch of covered stuff, but there was an AK-47 rifle visible. As he made a pass over the sampan, one of the VC worked the AK under the cover so it wouldn't be seen and it proceeded on down the river. The Cobra pilot kept his distance, so as not to arouse suspicion while awaiting permission to fire. He started to get excited because the permission was being delayed as the sampan was moving out of the grid square on towards Football Island. As it turned out, the sampan was faster than the permission to fire, and the pilot then started the procedure all over again for the new coordinates. By the time permission finally came to sink that sampan, the wary VC had beached the thing on Football Island and fled on foot. As I recall though, the pilot did light up the sampan when finally allowed. Of course, if those VC had shot at the Cobra, he could have made pillars of water out of that thing immediately. The VC were just little, but smart, definitely not just a little smart. I think it was our own American hierarchy that was just a little smart.

Another time, a recon team, just south of us in the Que Son mountains, was having to remain very quiet because enemy troops were searching for them. The RTO said he could smell them, then he would key the mike to maintain contact with the recon headquarters, rather than speak, even softly, into the mike to give a SitRep. Several minutes went by, then he started keying rapidly and I could hear gunfire every time he keyed. He started yelling into the mike, "Contact, Contact, Contact," and then silence for several minutes. The next time squelch was broken,

Looking south, this is a recon extract coming into An Hoa from the Que Son mountains, after a team had to be pulled out.

the RTO could be heard breathing very heavily. Finally, he announced that they were "on the move to an alternate harbor site, and were trying to break contact.

It was almost a daily occurrence to send in a spot report for infractions of some type or other, especially giving away locations in the clear. One afternoon, the Top came walking into our bunker after one of his weekly or so runs back to 1st Rad Bn Headquarters in DaNang. "Hey, Sgt Truitt, lookie here." Top Fitz had a compact, handheld directional antenna. The Top told me, "You need to find those jerks who go up on that BS net, and we'll try to get some of those guys off the air." "No sweat, Top, I'll take care of it." Wow, I was excited; something new! I started playing around with that "doo dah" immediately, and by evening I was on the trail of one of the Marines who was heard frequently on the BS net. The voice sounded familiar.

There I was, holding that little antenna out in front of me, following it like a carrot on a stick. Man, it was dark walking down the road from our area. That carrot on a stick led me all the way over into the 2nd Battalion's compound. Right into a hootch I went after that bozo mouthing off on the BS net. There wasn't even a .45 in my shoulder holster. Man, I was bold beyond belief. Shoot! I was a sergeant of Marines! Ha! No, that was really, really DUMB!

Hmmm, there was a bunch of grunts standing over near one side, laughing and cutting up with a guy sitting on a cot talking on a PRC-25. When they saw me standing there with the handheld antenna, there was complete silence.

All of a sudden—realization! I was in "deep, deep kimchee." Walking into that hootch with that antenna, everyone immediately looked at me as if I were wearing black pajamas, the common uniform of the Viet Cong. Instantly, my eyes caught the owner of the familiar voice, the RTO. With a big smile on my face, I stuck out my hand and walked toward him. "Hey BaraBara, how ya doing?" came from my lips. Joe Schmuckatelli quietly said he had a different girlfriend, though I could still see his Barabara tattoo. We slapped each other on the back a few times and shot the breeze for a little while before departing. "Shew!" that ComSec could be risky business!

As I look back at this, it makes me realize that there have been several times in my life—not just in Vietnam—when the situation could have quickly and easily led to my death. Once again, I have to say, Thank you, Jesus! Truly, He has been my Lord and my Savior ever since first asking Him to forgive me and inviting Him into my heart. That one action—based on the decision to trust in Jesus Christ who died for me, and rose again—was the pivotal point of my life, way back when I was just 13 years old!

DI DAH, DI DA DIT

25 Drop Your Drawers

"Okay people, let's get this show on the road." Slick, who was the organizer of this MedCap, was ready for us to get rolling.

There at An Hoa we had changed hootches several times. The last hootch that we 1st Rag Bag guys lived in collapsed one night in the spring of 1970. None of us were injured in any way, but it's an interesting experience to have your house shifting all around you in the middle of a pitch black night. We then moved

Joe Slick treating some children in Phu Da 1 (Duc Duc) on a MedCap before the communists slaughtered all the people and burnt the whole village.

into a hootch closer to our Ops bunker, which happened to be in the 5th Marine Regiment's 3rd Battalion area; must have been around the end of April. Our hootch was right next to a bunch of navy corpsmen. One of them was a long tall 2nd Class Petty Officer. He had a dark Fu Manchu mustache, but his name escapes me so I'll call him Joe Slick. Slick and I became pretty good friends. In fact, we went on R&R together to Sydney, Australia, later in June.

The BAS (battalion aid station) was right next to us—a heavily sandbagged bunker with a double roof. The top roof was elevated about a foot above the real sandbag roof, and it was made from corrugated sheetmetal to reflect the sun. Most importantly, it would serve to pre-detonate incoming artillery and mortar rounds. All the corpsman had put stretchers on the roof to lay out and work on their suntans. As a result their bottles of suntan lotion were all over the roof. What a way to run a war! But I started doing it too.

There was also a bin, next to the BAS, where Marines who were wounded would have their serviceable cammies deposited when they got medevaced back to DaNang. After awhile, every set of cammies I had came from the medevac bin; I'd just pick out the good ones, wash 'em and wear 'em. Slick was taking several of his corpsman to the village of Phu Da 1 for a MedCap (medical civil assistance program), and he asked me if I'd like to go along to help provide security. After everyone had gathered at the

It may not look like much here, but that water buffalo is a "mean Marine stomping machine."

BAS, Slick said loud and clear, "Okay people, let's get this show on the road." And we all climbed up into the back of a 6-by and proceeded out of the south gate by the 8" battery. As soon as you exit the gate you can go left or SE and be in Phu Da 3 immediately, but we made a hard right which took us through Phu Da 2, up to Phu Da 1 (also called Duc Duc) and the Song Tin Yen river (also called the Song Thu Bon after a deserted town just north in the Arizona Territory). That whole area was the TAOR of the enemy's 2nd NVA Division, and associated VC cadre.

This kid "dogged" me in the ville the whole time like he was on a mission; I'm glad he did!

MedCaps were exclusively to benefit the Vietnamese, but that particular village was no picnic. It was along the river at the edge of the Arizona Territory. Once a hotbed and where Marines had died in the past, it was presently friendly and had a nearby CAP team of Marines and ARVNs. Security—plenty of security—was an absolute must. I went on the MedCap for the change of pace, and it was enjoyable. My tour in Vietnam—and times just like that, while providing security there in Phu Da 1—certainly made me better appreciate the blessings that our Lord has bestowed on America.

Those villagers were ostensibly non-combatants, but some were VC sympathizers, either voluntarily or through coercion, torture and/ or murder, which was the normal communist mode of operation. Regardless, the result was the same; we tried to help them, but plenty of security was required as well. It was like trying to help an injured dog. You've gotta muzzle 'em before you can help 'em. All in all, that MedCap was uneventful, other than the VC water buffalo that chased me into the river. Ha! And don't ya know? those things are not afraid of water either. Here's a tip for you all. When chased by a VC water buffalo, don't bother to take refuge in the river. My salvation came in the form of a little boy, and an old man (who was struck with his share, and indeed the whole village's share of wrinkles all at one time).

According to a Marine Corps *Gazette* article of November 1989, by Major J. F. Jennings, several months after I was in Phu Da 1 for that MedCap, the Marines were pulled out of the area in accordance with President Nixon's Vietnamization plans. In March 1971, the communists went into Duc Duc village, slaughtered all the people and burnt the whole village to the ground.

Sometime after that MedCap with the demoniac water buffalo, I had received my next set of orders to the Marine detachment on the navy base at Edzell, Scotland. It so happens that my obligated time in the Corps was still another year after my tour in Vietnam was up. They told me that I'd spend that time on

A U/I Corpsman helping the children of Phu Da 1, all of whom would be slaughtered by the communists.

another unaccompanied tour unless I re-enlisted or extended to make it a three-year tour. That way I could have my wife and daughter with me the whole time. Well, I had done that already to get my tour at Homestead. I had extended for one year to have enough time for an accompanied tour because my wife was pregnant, and I didn't want to be away from her when the baby was born. So I did the extension for one year, received the orders to Homestead, my daughter was born and not too long thereafter I got orders to Vietnam. My total tour at Homestead was from August through May.

In all fairness to the Corps, I need to throw in a little caveat. After my daughter was born in December of 1968, I repeatedly went into the company office and volunteered for Vietnam. No, I think volunteered is not really honest either. I kinda begged to go. I was afraid I'd miss the chance, especially after we'd so completely discomfited the NVA militarily in their 1968 Tet offensive.

He saved me from the water buffalo; a year later he was slaughtered along with the whole village by the communists.

Phu Da 1 (Duc Duc) on the Song Thu Bon river.

Thus, I was aware of the ramifications of extending for a tour to Scotland, and my future plans still entertained thoughts of a commercial diving career. Then there was also the attraction of extending for six months in Vietnam which included a free 30-day leave to anywhere I wanted to go. I was really, really tempted, but since I had left the excitement of the northern "I" Corps area, things had gone downhill for me. It was definitely unremarkable there in An Hoa, and I completely despised my ComSec job. No, I decided to leave this banality. I'd re-enlist, take those orders in hand with my family and "tuff it out" in the bonnie land of Scotland for a three-year tour.

In order to re-up, I had to have a physical. Well, that was easy enough. I'd have that done right there at the BAS. A navy chief did most of the preliminaries, and a navy doctor did a couple things, then signed off on the forms. But while I was waiting, something took place that I thought was very interesting, and I'll never forget it. There were about a half-dozen Marines and several ARVNs that came filing into the bunker. The chief told them to line up about two feet out, and along one wall of the bunker. Then he said something like, "Okay, now turn around facing the wall and drop your drawers, then put your hands against the wall and lean into it." Hmmm, well that was certainly interesting. Man! what a compromising position.

Immediately thereafter a corpsman entered with a tray full of huge syringes filled with pale yellow, honey-looking stuff. As the one corpsman held the tray, another corpsman took a syringe in each hand and jammed both syringes into the buttocks of each man with his drawers dropped. That's a syringe in each cheek, and the stuff must have been pretty thick too, because it took some effort from the corpsman to squeeze it in. The chief was just laughing, but I assure you that there was no laughing against the wall. I couldn't laugh; I was kinda dumbstruck. Slick later, up on the roof soaking up the sun's rays, told me that those guys were a CAP team who had all been exposed to hepatitis, and that it was gamma gobulin in the needles. Whoa! They sure looked like horse needles to me, and a phrase that I frequently heard in Nam came to my mind once again, "Better him than me!"

Terry Wheeler, and John Dobre in the 1st Radio Battalion Ops. Bunker at An Hoa in the Spring of 1970.

Of note, a few years later I saw that navy chief again at the chief's club in Monterey, California, while a student at the language school. I was a guest of a retired army sergeant major, Harold Nanny. The chief once again laughed about that incident.

DI DAH, DI DA DIT

26 Mind Games

At An Hoa in the spring of 1970, the Marine's 175mm guns were at the north end of the runway and off to the east side. One day around April there was a short, but hard rainstorm, just as the 175s fired over our head into the Que Son mountains. One of those big artillery rounds detonated right over top of us. It made a big boom which was magnified downward by the cloud cover, and we had a large piece of shrapnel on top of our operations bunker. Little things like that happened periodically to break up the day-to-day monotony.

A 175mm gun

Sgt Truitt holding a 151-pound projectile.

Not too long after the MedCap to Phu Da 1, Top Fitzgerald and I made a run to Headquarters, 1st Radio Battalion in DaNang. "Hey, Top, do you mind if I take several cases of C-rations with us for trading material with those air force guys?" The Top said, "No problem, Sgt. Truitt, do you think a dozen cases will do it? I think, though, that I only took six or seven cases. Top and I climbed into the PC vehicle (a 3/4 ton personnel carrier) and headed up there. It was one of the few times I had been able to drive in Vietnam, even though I was the mechanical guy in the platoon and did all the maintenance on the vehicle. Who knows how long that PC had been around, but for sure it was a long time VietVet. As with many of the vehicles down south, one of the tricks we used to keep water in the radiator was to apply a spoonful of coarse ground pepper. A spoonful of that stuff every now and then would plug up any leaks in the cooling system, although a bullet hole in the radiator was a wee bit too much to expect, even from water-swollen, coarse ground pepper.

After driving up to DaNang and spending the day running around taking care of business—much of it personal—it was too

Davis, Santominio, and Stevens in front of a PC vehicle. —Courtesy of Bob Davis

late to make the trip back so we spent the night in DaNang. I had visited there several months earlier with my brother-in-law, who lived in a two-story barracks and worked in a nice air-conditioned building there. It was all completely enclosed in a large compound called Gunfighter Village. I'd had a three day in-country R&R to visit him, and it was a nice break. Those air force folks really knew how to make the best of it when far away from home! One major problem I had with going into their compound, though, was getting through their gate. Obviously, it was because I looked so much like a VC, they made me check my rifle in. I kinda had the feeling of going around with my zipper down; of course my zipper was broke anyhow, but I'm sure that you know what I mean. None of those AF guys had weapons, nor needed them because all of the guarding was handled by their specially trained security guys who did all that kind of stuff. Seemed to me that for most of them, it was like a regular job back in the States except they didn't have their wives with them.

I suppose that many of those folks never even left that compound during their whole tour down south. Actually, they didn't need to. They had everything there that they could ever need, such as a picnic area, a ball diamond and even a swimming pool. I mean they even had guys like me bringing them C-rations.

Previously, I had made a couple contacts there who would trade some really good stuff like food goodies and beverages for a case of C-rats. This time I was ready for those guards too. I gave them my M-16, but they never even knew about the .45 that was under my cammie jacket. When I headed back to 1st Rag Bag Headquarters, I had a lot of goodies and beverages, and I even kept a case of C's. DaNang could be a gold mine if I could've arranged to make regular weekly runs to there. Regrettably, it was just a one-time thing, though I'd been looking forward to it for several months since having visited there earlier. I didn't even get to see my brother-in-law that trip as he was working deep inside his air-conditioned Comm. Center building.

The next day, the Top and I headed back down to An Hoa. There were several vehicles heading south, but somehow we

A PC vehicle (personnel carrier). —Courtesy of Gary Haag

managed to be the last one and we stayed very spread out. We passed Hill 55 on the left and Hill 10 on the right, and continued on down. I'm not sure if we had passed Hill 37 or not, but for sure it was before Liberty Bridge that we saw many Vietnamese civilians in the street and all over the place.

That was the most civilians I'd seen at any one time in Vietnam, outside of a big city like DaNang or Hue. We were slowed to a crawl because of all the people everywhere, and the vehicle up ahead was far out of sight. I have no idea what the occasion was, but for sure something was happening. "What do you suppose is the deal with all of these people, Top?" Top said something like, "I don't know what is going on," and about that time we both heard a loud clunk, followed by a muffled bang, bang, right behind us in the back of the covered PC. We were just moving at a snail's pace and the Top yelled "grenade!" Immediately he was out of the door, rapidly moving away toward the side of the road. I hit the brakes and stopped. Now I'm going to tell you the events the way I remember them. You know, in times like that, things seem a little surreal. On the driver's side was a spare tire mounted on a bar that swung across the door. To exit the door, that lever had to be pulled first, then the regular handle had to be thrown to open the door. Since I had only driven that PC a couple times, I grabbed for the spare tire release to exit out of the driver's side. After a few seconds of fumbling, and things all in slow motion, I just stopped and sat there for what seemed like several minutes. All of a sudden there was the Top, right next to me, talking in my face. "Truitt, are you all right?" he asked. I have no idea what my words were. Then Top said, "I'm going to check in the back." He came back up front with an American, M-26 hand grenade. There was no pin in the fuse, but there were two wraps of black electrical tape going around the grenade holding the spoon securely in place.

Evidently, some malcontent gook was in that crowd intending to get revenge on an American for something or other.

1st RadBn's old French bunker at Hill 37. —Courtesy of Rick Swan

Seems like anyone with any training at all, such as a VC, would know that you gotta take the tape off the spoon as well as pull the pin. Everyone of my grenades was always taped. In fact, everybody I know taped their grenades, as well as partly bent the grenade pin back out so that it wouldn't be so hard to deal with when it was needed. I'd thrown several grenades up at FSB Fuller, but since moving down from the northern "I" Corps area, I never used any more weapons in anger. I mean, I didn't even threaten or shoot that demoniac water buffalo that chased me into the river back at Phu Da 1. Looking around, now there wasn't anybody within a hundred yards; they were just all of a sudden gone.

At Liberty Bridge we picked up two Marines who were needing a ride to An Hoa, but other than that, it was a pretty mundane ride. I don't even think we talked all the way back, except when the Top said to me, "If that grenade would have gone off, not only would you have been dead, but that whole area would have smelled a lot from all those bottles and cases of beverage that I see you traded for." (Actually, that's not precisely what he said, but I'm definitely not gonna repeat it!)

I've thought about that incident many times over the years, though I've told the story just a few times. I suppose I've wondered about the validity, and whether my mind has played tricks on me or not—that is, until just this past spring, 3 April 03, when communicating with Jake Bowditch, a former Marine staff sergeant who knew Harry Fitzgerald very well. Jake sent me the following, "Sorry to inform you that Master Sergeant Harry Fitzgerald passed away on November 26th, 2001...Harry was honored at the Marine Corps Ball in 2001 down at Camp Lejuene. He often spoke of the incident you mentioned." Harry sure was a good guy, and Jake Bowditch verified my story! So my mind hasn't been playing games with me. Thanks Jake, er Harry. But more than that, I want to thank Jesus Christ my Lord for saving me both physically and spiritually, in spite of my being

Vietnamese civilians in the street.

prone to wander. Looking ahead, He knew I'd be one of His ministers, and so I suppose He just planned on the extra effort to keep me kicking.

I'm not positive, but if my memory serves me correct, I think Harry unscrewed the fuse on that grenade and blew the cap. Then he put it all back together again, tape and all—minus the pin—then set it up in our Ops bunker as a reminder to the two of us. Hmmm, did that really happen or is my mind playing tricks on me?

DI DAH, DI DA DIT

27 The Face-off

On the 4th of July, it was necessary to do something extraordinary. After thinking on it, my plan was to do what I did on New Year's Eve at Dong Ha just before going back up to FSB Fuller, except on a larger scale. My abilities to scrounge were pretty good, and even though they were a lot more difficult to acquire, somehow eight red and seven green pop-up star clusters managed to appear. On the eve of July 4th I laid two boards out in front of me, one at either hand. The pop-ups were prepared by moving the caps to the opposite end so that all that was necessary was to grab them and smack each one down, hard onto

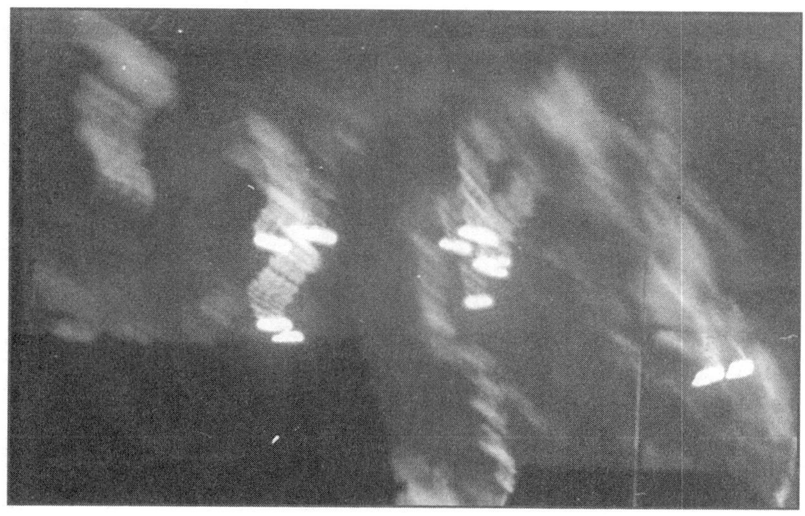

An Hoa, 4 July 70, star clusters—15 at one time.

the board. They were all prepped and laid out in an order, easy to grab. The green star clusters were on the right and the red on the left, just like the marker colors when departing a port. It was somewhere around 2000 or 2100 hours, a few hundred feet over An Hoa, RVN, that America's independence was celebrated with a beautiful red and green fireworks display. By grabbing a pop-up in each hand, and then smacking them both down at the same time, a red and a green could be launched in concert. Within 15 to 20 seconds, there were 15 star clusters up all at once. At Dong Ha, there were only ten up at once. I loved it!

My 21st birthday was on the 22nd of July, and just a week or so later was my last night in An Hoa. That night we were gassed with CS. Most of our 1st Platoon were playing cards when the first of the acrid fumes wafted across our noses. We just kinda looked at each other, waiting for it to blow by as in times past. Everyone thought no sweat, and like the few other times we'd just "gut out" the slight discomfort. But it just kept getting stronger and stronger. The round must have landed real close to our hootch, though we heard nothing. My mind was screaming

A typical street scene, possibly deadly. Courtesy Rob Charnell

with the knowledge that I had already packed my gas mask in the bottom of my WP bag in preparation for my departure for DaNang the following morning. We all looked at each other again for just an instant, then like a Chinese fire drill, there was a mass scramble on everyone's part for their gas masks.

That was miserable; they got me good that time. When I ran out of our hootch towards the Ops bunker, where I knew there was an extra mask hanging on the wall, I ran right out into a heavy cloud of the gas. Falling onto the ground coughing, sputtering and gagging, I crawled for a little ways until some unknown Gunny grabbed me by the collar and pulled me up out of that little benjo ditch I had fallen into. I couldn't see. Snot, mucus, saliva and mud covered my face. He dragged me to some hootch and handed me a mask. I still remember the misery—it was by far the worst gassing I'd ever had, far worse than any gas chamber or training I had received. All my training experiences after that were just a joke, comparatively.

The next day I made my last long trip up the road from An Hoa to DaNang. That was a miserable ride in the PC. My mind

This is Hill 37 between An Hoa and DaNang. 1st Rag Bag's area was where the old French bunker was at about five o'clock in the picture

This is a PC vehicle of the type 1st Plt, 1st RadBn used for transport. There was a bar and spare tire across the driver's door on the other side.

was full of thoughts of getting blown away on my way home. I remember little else until being at the terminal to leave on the jet plane.

All of a sudden, I remembered the face-off from a year earlier when I had arrived in this same terminal. This time I was watching the NUGs, the new guys, as they were arriving in-country. This time I was one of those tanned guys awaiting my turn to board the same aircraft that they had just flown in on. I wondered how many of them wouldn't make it at all, and this time I wondered how many would be physically and mentally changed for the rest of their life.

The Chuck Truitt that boarded that plane was a certainly a lot different from the one who'd been in that group of NUGs a year ago, and the original number was much less too. My year in Vietnam was the second highest in total casualties of the Vietnam war; I was not one of them.

I think it was the 30th or 31st of July when our Freedom Bird roared down the runway. Shortly after the wheels lifted off, there was a slight sinking lurch and then somebody started cheering. Within about a half second, there was a whole plane load of guys cheering and whistling, and then complete silence all the way to Okinawa. I suppose those contracted stewardesses who flew that leg of the flight thought we were the biggest bunch of deadbeats that ever left Vietnam.

The Marine Corps took everyone leaving Vietnam to Okinawa for five days. I was with a bunch of other guys in a Quonset hut at Camp Hague. It's no longer there now though. In fact, there is a MacDonalds where the entrance to the camp was, but the little tree-topped hill, with the Japanese shrine on it, is still there. It was an interesting first morning completely away from Vietnam. About 100 to 150 guys were standing in formation at 0700 in front of the Quonset huts when some jerk threw a string of firecrackers right behind us. Every Marine immediately hit the deck in place. Within a couple hours I was in the tailor shop at the entrance to the Camp Hague gate being measured for a new, three- piece suit, all 145 pounds of a lean, mean-as-a-snake, me. It sure was a nice tailormade suit, but I was never able to fit into it again.

After the five days in Okinawa, the Marine Corps took us back to California, and we made our own transportation arrangements from there. I had about a month's leave before needing to report, with my family, for a flight to Scotland. There I was at the airport with my tropical summer uniform and sergeant's chevrons; I went to the Delta counter and said, "I need to get a ticket on the next bird to Ft. Lauderdale." Two guys stood behind the ticket counter—one was older and dumpy and one was tall. Both were wearing black trousers and a white shirt, and both spoke to me and handled themselves toward me in a very rude manner. The tall guy said (among other things), "We don't fly any birds out of here." Evidently, those folks had fallen in with much of the rest of the nation in welcoming home her veterans. There were probably two

At the airport, seeing my daughter for the first time since she was six months old. After my tour in Vietnam, August '70, I was down to 145 pounds, and 6 feet tall, but I had a great tan.

things that kept me from jumping that counter and ramming my .45 up his nose. First was the thought of my wife and infant daughter awaiting me in Ft. Lauderdale, and secondly was the fact that my .45 was still back in Vietnam serving our country. "Welcome Home, Marine." I've had a bad taste in my mouth towards those people ever since.

I did get a flight that morning, bright and early too. It was the 6th of August, 1970. The plane was completely empty in the whole backend. After stretching out and immediately falling asleep, the next thing I remember was seeing the Everglades on approach into the Ft. Lauderdale airport. "Wow, can you believe all that construction west of State Road 7? It was all swamps and orange groves just a year ago."

Linda, and my 20-month-old daughter Marie, met me at the airport. It was Linda's 21st birthday, and Marie immediately came into my arms.

DA DI DAH, DI DAH, DI DA DIT

28 Through a Glass, Darkly

Do you ever just lie in bed and think about things? Well, I do. We've squeezed a lot of orange juice since my departure from Vietnam way back in 1970.

A few days ago, actually it was the wee hours of the morning, Linda and I were lying in bed thinking and talking about getting older. Linda said to me, "Do you feel any skinnier?" "What are you talking about, Linda? Then my little wife said something like, "As I lay here in the dark, I feel pretty skinny. How about you?" Now don't get me wrong, Linda is not fat, but neither is she the 96 pounder that I married. Of course, I too weigh a little more than I did when I left the Marine Corps at 175 pounds in 1981. Actually, I had gotten the maximum of 300 points on the Marine PFT (physical fitness test) just 10 days before leaving the Corps so I was in excellent physical condition. As I said, there's

Chuck and Linda Truitt a few months ago. Heh, heh! Well, maybe a little longer than that!

been a lot of orange juice squeezed. I had to admit to Linda that I did feel kind of skinny just laying there at "oh-dark-thirty" with all the lights off. I couldn't see the real me. Linda also said, "Don't you feel young again?" Well, she may have gotten over that pretty quick about the time I fell back asleep and started snoring, since I didn't ever snore when I was younger.

That's a lot like everyone's picture of our own lives. God's Word says, "For now we see through a glass darkly…" We surely don't have a clear picture of things, and what we see and know is certainly just in part; we have false views of ourselves. That's also the way most folks view themselves concerning salvation and what God says concerning eternal life. We don't necessarily think of ourselves as being bad enough to go to hell, but, God says "There is none righteous, no, not one: there is none that understandeth, there is none that seeketh after God." He also says, "For all have sinned and come short of the glory of God."

Awhile ago I read about a guy who committed suicide some place in the frozen North. He had been stranded and was out of food and freezing to death. They found him after the deed was done, and he had a written a note asking the Lord to forgive him

as the suicide was possibly the only sin he had ever committed. Boy, did he ever miss what God plainly said in His Word, the Bible. You see, even if I lived a perfect life from the time I was born, I am still a sinner as a result of sin coming into the world when Adam sinned in the Garden of Eden. I was born breaking the greatest commandment as Jesus said, "Thou shalt love the Lord thy God with all thy heart, and with all thy soul, and with all thy mind."

I often lay in bed and think about my friends, and my acquaintances, folks I have come in contact with over the years. I suppose the biggest thing I think about is whether or not I'll see them again.

I met and became friendly with a bunch of guys in Vietnam, but of them all, the Greek is the one I was closest to. I sure do hope that he realized what God said about our sins, "For the wages of sin is death; but the gift of God is eternal life through Jesus Christ our Lord." If Greek, and indeed all my friends and acquaintances, grasped what the Bible says, "For by grace are ye saved through faith; and not of yourselves: it is a gift of God: Not of works, lest any man should boast" and what Jesus said, "I am the way, the truth, and the life: no man cometh unto the Father, but by me," then they may have trusted in Jesus Christ for salvation.

Sometimes we can be looking at something and not see it, and then sometimes we can be looking for something and still not see it. A few months ago—heh, heh—well, maybe longer ago than that, I was driving down the road on I-10 just west of Pensacola, Florida, on a bright and sunny afternoon. Linda looked over at me from the passenger seat and noticed from that angle that there was a bunch of grime and nastiness on my glasses which I had been looking through for quite some time. She said, "Chuck, hand me your glasses so I can clean them off." After she did her handiwork, I put them back on my face and

wow, what a difference. I didn't even realize all I had been missing until I got my glasses cleaned.

That's what it's like with eternal salvation. Most people are going around with dirty glasses, either not concerned about salvation or working for salvation in some way or another. They don't even realize what they're missing, as the Bible says, "The god of this world hath blinded the minds of them which believe not." Most folks need to get their glasses cleaned. How about you? Maybe you need your glasses cleaned too.

Why don't you just take God at His Word, and trust that Jesus shed His precious blood—not for himself, but for us, to pay for our sins. "Without the shedding of blood is no remission [of sin]." Jesus did it! He came to this earth and took on the form of a man in order to shed His blood for us. We need His shed blood applied to our sins, and that happens just by asking, "For whosoever shall call upon the name of the Lord shall be saved."

Why don't you trust in and ask Jesus Christ to save you right now?

"And I thank Christ Jesus our Lord, who hath enabled me, for that he counted me faithful, putting me into the ministry" (1 Timothy 1:12).

OPINION VS. KNOWLEDGE

By Jim Baxter
Sgt USMC- WWII and Korea

"There are only two groups of people
who know U.S. Marines:
1. U.S. Marines,
and 2. the enemy.
Everybody else has a secondhand opinion."

SEMPER FIDELIS—ALWAYS FAITHFUL

CHUCKIE
BY KUDYARD RIPLING

I went into a public-'ouse to get a pint o' beer,
The publican 'e up an' sez, "We serve no redcoats here."
The girls be'ind the bar they laughed an' giggled fit to die,
I outs into the street again an' to myself sez I:
O it's Chuckie this, an' Chuckie that, an' "Chuckie, go away";
But it's "Thank you, Mister Truitt," when the band begins to play,—
The band begins to play, my boys, the band begins to play,
O it's "Thank you, Mister Truitt," when the band begins to play.

I went into a theatre as sober as could be,
They gave a drunk civilian room, but 'adn't none for me;
They sent me to the gallery or round the music-'alls,
But when it comes to fightin', Lord! they'll shove me in the stalls!
For it's Chuckie this, an' Chuckie that, an' "Chuckie, wait outside;"
But it's "special train for Truitt" when the trooper's on the tide,—
The troopship's on the tide, my boys, the troopship's on the tide,
O it's "special train for Truitt" when the trooper's on the tide.

Yes, makin' mock o' uniforms that guard you while you sleep
Is cheaper than them uniforms, an' they're starvation cheap;
An' hustlin' drunken soldiers when they're goin' large a bit
Is five times better business than paradin' in full kit.
Then it's Chuckie this, an' Chuckie that,
an' "Chuckie, 'ow's yer soul?"
But it's "thin red line of 'eroes" when the drums begin to roll,—
The drums begin to roll, my boys, the drums begin to roll,
O it's "thin red line of 'eroes" when the drums begin to roll.

We aren't no thin red 'eroes, nor we aren't no blackguards too,
But single men in barracks, most remarkable like you;
An' if sometimes our conduct isn't all your fancy paints,
Why, single men in barracks don't grow into plaster saints;
While it's Chuckie this, an' Chuckie that, an' "Chuckie, fall be'ind,"
But it's "Please to walk in front, sir,"
when there's trouble in the wind,—
There's trouble in the wind, my boys, there's trouble in the wind,
O it's "Please to walk in front, sir," when there's trouble in the wind.

You talk o' better food for us, an' schools, an' fires, an' all:
We'll wait for extry rations if you treat us rational.
Don't mess about the cook-room slops, but prove it to our face
The widow's uniform is not the soldierman's disgrace.
For it's Chuckie this, an' Chuckie that,
an' "Chuck him out, the brute!"
But it's "saviour of 'is country" when the guns begin to shoot;
An' it's Chuckie this, an' Chuckie that, an' anything you please;
An' Chuckie ain't a bloomin' fool—you bet that Chuckie sees!

Eternal Father grant we pray,
To all Marines both night and day.
The courage, honor, strength, and skill,
Their land to serve, Thy law fulfill.
Be now the shield forever more,
From every peril to the corps.

About the Author

Jesus Christ! I say that not in profanity, but in praise. Before my name is mentioned I want His name, who is God and Savior, proclaimed.

Named Wesley Charles Truitt at birth in July 1949. My life has been extraordinary. I met a beautiful girl (Linda) in high school, and have now had the privilege of having her for my wife for over 35 years. Having been in 34 countries and 46 states, it has also been my privilege to raise two children, a boy and a girl, and to have four grandchildren so far. To many things I can truly say, "been there, done that," including nearly 14 years in the U.S. Marine Corps, the last three as a gunnery sergeant. I am also a scuba diving Master Instructor, and have dove in many places around the world. Of it all, the most important and most life-changing was that evening church service, at only 13 years old, when I trusted in, and asked Jesus Christ to save me. Since that time many things have transpired, but it is my firm belief that the only things that will count positively for all eternity is

The Author, Chuck Truitt, in the Fall of 1969.

what I have done for Jesus Christ, especially the people I have influenced for Christ. There is an oriental saying that goes something like this:

He who cultivates for a little while cultivates rice.
He who cultivates for awhile cultivates trees.
But he who cultivates for a long while cultivates men.

In 1981 Linda and I departed Okinawa, Japan (my last tour of duty as a Marine) and began studying for full-time Christian service at Tennessee Temple University in Chattanooga, Tennessee. It was there that a burden to return as a missionary to Okinawa was implanted into my heart. Linda said she'd follow me anywhere. We have served now on Okinawa for 17 years as missionaries. I have been the pastor to hundreds of military folks and some Okinawans. Several of them are now pastors and missionaries themselves. It is my desire that this book, along with being interesting and enjoyable for anyone who reads it, will also inspire some towards the Savior.

"Only one life 'twill soon be past,
Only what's done for Christ will last."

Pop a Yellow Smoke
Order Form

Postal orders: Hessische Str. 110A
68305 Mannheim, Germany

Telephone orders: 01149 621 764 4878

E-mail orders: truittwc@aol.com

Please send *Pop a Yellow Smoke* to:

Name: ____

Address: ____

City: ___________________________ State: ____________

Zip: ______________ Telephone: (_____) ______________

Book Price: $16.95

Shipping: $3.00 for the first book and $1.00 for each additional book to cover shipping and handling within US, Canada, and Mexico. International orders add $6.00 for the first book and $2.00 for each additional book.

Or order from:
ACW Press
1200 HWY 231 South #273
Ozark, AL 36360

(800) 931-BOOK

or contact your local bookstore